PENGUIN INTERNATIONAL POETS

CHILD OF EUROPE

Michael March was born in 1946 in New York. After graduating in history from Columbia College, he left for Europe. He is the author of *Goya* and *Disappearance*, the co-translator of Zbigniew Herbert's *Barbarian in the Garden* and Gojko Djogo's *Ovid in Tomis*, for which he received a Translators Fellowship from the National Endowment for the Arts. He is the creator of the East European Forum, opened by President Václav Havel, at the Institute of Contemporary Arts in London. As an editor, he established the first list in British publishing devoted to East European literature. He is currently writing *Versions of the Truth*, journeys through Europe.

D0902044

Child of Europe

A NEW ANTHOLOGY OF EAST EUROPEAN POETRY

EDITED BY
MICHAEL MARCH

PENGUIN BOOKS

PENGUIN BOOKS

Published by the Penguin Group
Penguin Books Ltd, 27 Wrights Lane, London W8 5TZ, England
Viking Penguin, a division of Penguin Books USA Inc.
375 Hudson Street, New York, New York 10014, USA
Penguin Books Australia Ltd, Ringwood, Victoria, Australia
Penguin Books Canada Ltd, 2801 John Street, Markham, Ontario, Canada L3R 1B4
Penguin Books (NZ) Ltd, 182–190 Wairau Road, Auckland 10, New Zealand

Penguin Books Ltd, Registered Offices: Harmondsworth, Middlesex, England

This selection first published 1990
1 3 5 7 9 10 8 6 4 2

This selection copyright © Michael March, 1990
All rights reserved

The acknowledgements on page 249 constitute an extension of this copyright page

Printed in England by Clays Ltd, St Ives plc
Filmset in Monophoto Photina

The Times Literary Supplement featured 'New Poems from 8 East European Countries' in
celebration of the 'Child of Europe' readings at the South Bank Centre, London, on 24–5
February 1990. The poems were: 'Absence', Wolfgang Hilbig; 'The beginnings crossed out',
Ryszard Krynicki; 'Her little red ear', Ioana Crăciunescu; 'Winter of 1968', György Petri;
'Valley of the roses', Lyubomir Nikolov; 'Black tiger', Sylva Fischerová; 'To a serving girl',
Elena Shvarts; 'The black sheep', Gojko Djogo.

FOR HANNA

CONTENTS

EAST GERMANY

ROMANIA

YUGOSLAVIA

THE SOVIET UNION

THE BALTIC REPUBLICS

ESTONIA

DORIS KAREVA

LITHUANIA

SIGITAS GEDA

LATVIA

JURIS KUNNOSS

PREFACE

With one exception, the poets in *Child of Europe* were born after 1940 and grew up in communist regimes. Without exception, their voice is unique and will not be repeated in history. I must confess that I have discovered no rules attached to their voice. I simply drew a line at the Urals and insisted that the poets stay at home. It is my wish to transmit a part of their speech.

I hesitate to attach 'revolution' to the recent events in Eastern Europe, for the ancient proverb 'Conduct your triumph as a funeral' still remains fresh. The Czech poet Vladimír Holan wrote, 'Freedom is always kin to voluntary poverty,' and we still await the answer. In Eastern Europe poets are accountants. Their ledgers contain the unprofitability of the human soul. When János Pilinszky said, 'The earth betrays me in its embrace, the rest is grace,' he replaced history with poetry.

In Eastern Europe humour often replaces tragedy. Franz Kafka, the first modern weatherman, was an impossible romantic. For him the poet's song was a scream: 'Art for the artist is only suffering, through which he releases himself to further suffering.' His stoker is now foreign minister in this 'single great life in which we take part'.

Since *The Epic of Gilgamesh*, the poet has sown the fields of immortality. He has learned little save that immortality is the highest form of madness. He is left with his word broken into life, living in contradiction. The poet lives with the taste of death in his mouth, though his *attempt* is a thing of rare beauty.

By the time of the Fifth Psalm, poets had learned to dismiss ideology.

> There is no faithfulness in their mouth,
> and their inner parts are destruction;
> their throat is an open grave,
> and all their tongues are smooth.

What remains is Rimbaud's dictum: 'Spiritual combat is as brutal as the battle between men.'

As the Seventies wore on, the young generation of East European poets matured. Their rise met the fall of the state. Their visibility coincided with the political movements of the times: KOR and Solidarity in Poland and Charter 77 in Czechoslovakia. Their actions were both natural and traditional, and their words were spread through *samizdat*.

> Write so the hungry
> think it is bread?
>
> The hungry should be fed.
> One should write so that hunger
> would not be in vain.
> Ryszard Krynicki

I fear materialism, not censorship. When I lived in Warsaw, during the first spring of Solidarity, the Writers' Union fought the Ministry of Culture over my meat coupons. Words took second place. Communist regimes were ripe for poetry. They even printed it at their own expense. There were numerous literary journals, and young poets were published. Censorship was not acceptable, never enviable; but it was recognizable. With the lessening of borders, materialism will replace longing and poetry will suffer.

Our words are not immortal, but their spirit survives. It is natural to preserve our name, to preserve the true independence of states. 'Attention is the natural prayer of the soul.' God bless the child that listens.

INTRODUCTION

It's raining now, but then I was in West Berlin with Zbigniew Herbert. In his cubicle. His reformatory. His home at the Akademie der Kunst. I remember trying to find him. No one had heard of him. Finally a guard pointed upwards. Herbert sat alone, drinking. Smiling. Engaging me with a mock Californian accent. No, I don't like sea-lions. Later singing old Polish songs as his wife knotted his tie and drove an old Volkswagen towards a New Year's Eve party through red lights towards the zoo.

I remember Berlin that night. Exploding, hypnotic, a cascade of fireworks. And in the morning, overcoats strewn about an empty room. Fur coats. The streets strewn with rubbish. I remember the Polish poets, the Polish community. Herbert, Wirpsza, Karpowicz. Each complaining about each other. Each reclaiming stolen lines. Each a terrible exile. Dog-paddling. Thirty years after the war.

Forget about the old men and think about the children. Where does one enter Eastern Europe? And once inside, can one visibly leave?

I started in Poland. I came looking for a dead child, the child placed in the shallow grave of prophecy by Czesław Miłosz in his poem 'Child of Europe'. Fortunately, the body does not beat without a heart.

It took months, even years. Let's say twenty years. I was in Warsaw. At the Warsaw Book Fair. Looking at the poverty of books. Looking at the immensity of books. Seeing the North Koreans, the Vietnamese, our Chinese brothers and Russian sisters. There was no room for banned poetry. Let's say it came to me there.

Miłosz wrote 'Child of Europe' in 1946, in New York, while he was cultural attaché at the Polish Embassy in Washington. A profound poem, its cynicism still lights the evening sky. It was written in the year of my birth and heralds a new age.

> The voice of passion is better than the voice of reason.
> The passionless cannot change history.

I had wished to use these lines for my 'Child of Europe' readings at the South Bank in London but was scolded by Erich Fried, the great Austrian poet who lived unmolested in Kilburn while commuting to Germany. Had I missed the Enlightenment? The readings were dedicated to his memory: 'I wanted to be the banner of my time or a shred of its banner.'

In Eastern Europe the prophets have perished: Mandelstam prowling Voronezh in his blue shoes; Celan listening to his 'mutilated music'; Nichita Stănescu calling himself 'the ridiculous mute' and singing Romanian folksongs into the black Macedonian night.

> Do not love people: people soon perish.
> Or they are wronged and call for your help.

I am sitting at a table with Djogo, Nikolov, Fisherová, and Krynicki in a Greek restaurant near the British Museum. Music, red wine, cigarettes. Food is a magic weapon for words. This is their first night in London, two nights before the readings at the South Bank. For the moment, they rejoice without understanding our one-party state.

Gojko Djogo tells the story that after he was jailed the guards couldn't believe that such a nice person could be thrown inside. This did not prevent him from being forced to share a cell with convicted murderers or help his bleeding ulcer. Djogo was the first Yugoslav writer to be imprisoned for poetry in over a century. The most civil. In 1981 he received a two-year sentence for publishing *Woolly Times*, a collection of verse in which the prosecutor recognized the slim figure of Tito.

> And he lies dead now
> and insane animals lick his paws,
> cattle are distrustful of their snouts:
> he is not dead, but silent?

Lyubomir Nikolov is clearly amused. He has been amused since arriving and will be amused throughout his stay. Just don't ask him to be on time. Reading most Bulgarian poets is like living on Death Row. But this bear is a lifeguard. In a country where everything must appear solid, he used 'perhaps' in a poem and lived. In 1987 his second collection of verse, *Traveller*, caused a minor tremor in literary circles. How on earth could a wrestler possess the sensibilities of an oriental tea ceremony?

> Water flowing down the stone,
> a lizard flitting through the grass.
> What prayer can bring you such
> sweet freedom for your soul?
> Go and become one this day
> with the grass, the stone, the water:
> from the slavery of the senses
> liberated for all time.

Sylva Fischerová is seated to my right. She has been to Greece and lived on a beach with cheap red wine. This is the closest that she has come to the Elgin Marbles. Sylva is tired after her flight from Prague but livens up with black olives. In Prague there are demonstrations demanding Havel's release from prison. She studies Greek and Latin and smokes Zeus cigarettes to infinity. She is the finest Czech poet since the Prague Spring, when she was a child.

> Sometimes it's enough to put out the light
> and sit
>   in the night blue
>   as the tremor of racehorses.
>   But what if their tremor is green?
>   What if it's brown?

I have known Ryszard Krynicki since the birth of Solidarity. He lives on the outskirts of Poznań, tucked into a housing estate that is not far from the mud huts of Abyssinia. There are no telephones or shops. He always carries a large leather shoulder bag filled with contraband books, unposted letters and slices of ham. During martial law he was beaten by detectives for his close association with the dissident movement. Krynicki is the key figure of the 'New Wave', the generation of '68 that realistically portrayed the infirmities and corruption in communist Poland. By nature he is extremely reticent. His recent work is close to the poetry of Celan, whom he translated along with Nelly Sachs. His poems are sparse, delicate meditations that alight as prayers.

> It was my fortune to overcome fear:
> I didn't sign the loyalty oath
> – and yet I am free. Free?
> My hour of trial
>
> nears.

It is becoming clear that the Romanian poet Ioana Crăciunescu won't be allowed out. Throughout the week there have been signals. The Romanian authorities have lied again.

Ioana is another story. I saw her big black boots in Belgrade and knew, from a distance, that she had to be a fine poet. But security was tight, and I was fighting to salvage an omelette from invisible waiters.

> The rat runs through the streets, not a boot touches it.
> There's poison about.
> Ah, sings the poison, small and grey is my body now.

György Petri arrives. He's hidden by his clothes. He looks older than I expected, and I wouldn't dare put a match to his breath. I'm told that he needs to be watched. What does that mean? He won't take off his wide-brimmed hat. He won't mix. For years Petri has been the protruding vein of Hungarian poetry. For years he has refused official publication, preferring the infra-red world of *samizdat* literature. He has visibly suffered.

> Because of disgust, because it all sticks in my craw,
> revenge has become my dream and my daily bread.
> And this revulsion is stronger than the gods.
> I already see how mould is creeping across Mycenae,
> which is the mould of madness and destruction.

Elena Shvarts arrives. She has come as a 'delegation' from Leningrad. A classless gesture made by the writers' union, but she's here, rather in a state of shock from her first taste of foreign soil.

She is in black, punctuated by a minute pair of black plastic boots.
My first reaction is to kiss her hand.

> To teach the mouth once more the patience of an object,
> How to bind knots and not decipher them.

During the 'years of stagnation', her generation kept literature
alive through the pages of *samizdat* journals and in the émigré
press. She has had many poetical personae from God-crazed nun
to mistress of Sextus Propertius. For the moment, she is with-
drawn.

That leaves Wolfgang Hilbig from East Germany to complete
the circle of poets for the readings. There's a message to the effect
that Hilbig won't show. The word used is 'obstacles'. What 'ob-
stacles' could there be for Wolfgang? I ring his West German
editor. He's hung up on finishing his novel. I play the ace. Hilbig
will never be published in the English language unless he gets
here. Wolfgang arrives on time.

> when at noon the shore is gleaming
> and stones float upward like cork . . .
> green from the rubble of your gates flocks to you

Hilbig is short and distant. He worked as a labourer in Leipzig and
remains a glazier of words, his work virtually unknown in his
home. I see him through a dark mirror in a rented room.

That these readings exist is a miracle. In former times some of
these poets were banned, threatened and jailed. In former times
'Child of Europe' was a poem written by an unknown poet. Now
we shall profit from the benevolence of former antagonists to
witness a family reunion.

ACKNOWLEDGEMENTS

Working with poets, disguised as translators, has its own alchemy. I am grateful to the translators for their dedication and patience.

May I lend my sympathy to the memory of Erich Fried and George Theiner.

Kind regards to R. S. Thomas, who doesn't believe in translation.

I wish to thank Paul-Eerik Rummo and the writers' union of the Baltic republics, the Bulgarian Writers' Union, the Czech Ministry of Culture, the Polish Cultural Institute in London, and the British Council for their assistance.

'What gives light must endure burning.'

Michael March
London, June 1990

HUNGARY

GYÖRGY PETRI

György Petri was born in 1943 in Budapest. He worked in various jobs, including a work-therapy institute for the mentally ill, before studying philosophy and psychology at the University of Budapest. After a stunning debut in the early 1970s, his politically outspoken, bitterly sarcastic and unconventional poetry remained unpublished for the next fifteen years in Hungary. Through *samizdat* he became the leading voice in new Hungarian poetry. In 1989 two collections, *It Exists Somewhere* and *Whatever was Left Out*, sold out on publication.

By an unknown poet from Eastern Europe, 1955

It's fading,
           like the two flags that, year by year,
we'd put out for public holidays
in the iron sheaths stuck over the gate –
like them the world's looking pale, it's fading now.

Where have they gone, the days of pomp and cheer?

Smothered with dust
in the warmth
of the attic room,
a world dismantled holds its peace.

The march has gone and disappeared.

It metamorphosed into a howl
the wind winnowed.
And now, instead of festive poets here,
the wind will recite into thin air,

it will utter scurrying dust and pulsating heat
above the concrete square.

That our women have been loved seems quite incredible.

Above the era
of taut ropes and white-hot foundries,
the tentative, wary
present – dust settling – hovers.

Above unfinished buildings:
imperial frauds, fantasies.

I no longer believe
what I believed once.
But the fact that I have believed –
that I compel myself
day by day to recall.

And I do not forgive anyone.

Our terrible loneliness
crackles and flakes
like the rust on iron rails in the heat of the sun.

Gratitude

The idiotic silence of state holidays
is no different
from that of Catholic Sundays.
People in collective idleness
are even more repellent
than they are when purpose has harnessed them.

Today I will not
in my old ungrateful way
let gratuitous love decay in me.
In the vacuum of streets
what helps me to escape
is the memory of your face and thighs,
your warmth,
the fish-death smell of your groin.

You looked for a bathroom in vain.
The bed was uncomfortable
like a roof ridge.
The mattress smelt of insecticide,
the new scent of your body mingling with it.

I woke to a cannonade
(a round number of years ago
something happened). You were still asleep.
Your glasses, your patent-leather bag
on the floor, your dress on the window-catch,
hung inside out – so practical.

One strap of your black slip
had slithered off.
And a gentle light was wavering
on the downs of your neck, on your collarbones,
as the cannon went on booming

and on a spring poking through
the armchair's cover
fine dust was trembling.

Electra

What *they* think is that it's the twists and turns of politics
that keep me ticking; they think it's Mycenae's fate.
Take my little sister, cute, sensitive Chrysosthemis –
to me the poor thing attributes a surfeit of moral passion,
believing I'm unable to get over
the issue of our father's twisted death.
What do I care for that gross geyser of spunk
who murdered his own daughter! The steps into the bath
were slippery with soap – and the axe's edge too sharp.
But that this Aegisthus, with his trainee-barber's face,
should swagger about and hold sway in this wretched town,
and that our mother, like a venerably double-chinned old whore,
should dally with him, simpering – everybody pretending
not to see, not to know anything. Even the Sun
glitters above, like a lie forged of pure gold,
the false coin of the gods!
Well, that's why! That's why! Because of disgust, because it all
        sticks in my craw,
revenge has become my dream and my daily bread.
And this revulsion is stronger than the gods.
I already see how mould is creeping across Mycenae,
which is the mould of madness and destruction.

To be said over and over again

I glance down at my shoe and – there's the lace!
This can't be gaol then, can it, in that case.

Night song of the personal shadow

The rain is pissing down,
you scum.
And you, you are asleep
in your nice warm room –
that or stuffing the bird.
Me? Till six in the morning
I rot in the slackening rain.
I must wait for my relief, I've got to wait
till you crawl out of your hole,
get up from beside your old woman.
So the dope can be passed on
as to where you've flown.
You are flying, spreading your wings.
Don't you get into my hands –
I'll pluck you while you're in flight.
This sodding rain
is something I won't forget,
my raincoat swelling
double its normal weight
and the soles of my shoes.
While you
were arsing around
in the warm room.

The time will come
when I feed you to fish in the Danube.

To Imre Nagy

You were impersonal, too, like the other leaders,
bespectacled, sober-suited; your voice lacked
sonority, for you didn't know quite what to say

on the spur of the moment to the gathered multitude. This urgency
was precisely the thing you found strange. I heard you,
old man in pince-nez, and was disappointed,
not yet to know

of the concrete yard where most likely the prosecutor
rattled off the sentence, or
of the rope's rough bruising, the ultimate shame.

Who can say what you might have said
from that balcony? Butchered opportunities, it is certain,
never return. Neither prison nor death
can resharpen the cutting edge of the moment

once it's been chipped. What we can do, though, is remember
the hurt, reluctant, hesitant man
who none the less soaked up
anger, delusion
and a whole nation's blind hope,

when the town woke to gunfire
that blew it apart.

Petri: translated from the Hungarian by Clive Wilmer and George Gömöri.

ZSUZSA RAKOVSZKY

Zsuzsa Rakovszky was born in 1950 in Budapest and currently works as a translator of English literature. In 1980 she won the Robert Graves Award for the best poem of the year by a young author. *Prophecies and Deadlines* was published in 1981, and *One House Further Away* appeared in 1987. Her poems focus on the patchwork of flesh and spirit and express a desperate, sensuous, heightened appreciation of life.

Snapshot

August   Balcony   Six p.m.
It's getting dark now   I am happy
and not happy   The horizontals
freeze in their flight   The deep perspective
draws me downwards   I am happy
and I am not   The rows of houses opposite
cast a shadow that's slipped across the road
and is now gradually climbing up the wall
over on this side   One by one it snuffs
the green vernal glows in the stone mugs
on neighbouring balconies   I am happy
and I am not   And now let nothing oh let nothing
happen   In me the carefully
poised surface of water
which has no wish to reflect anything now
but immaculate void would be shattered   I am happy
and I am not I am and I am not
and I am happy and

Noon

Less than a half-hour since
your skin was on mine, bare,
the spume of love-making still
in the shell of our flesh folds:
my two feet to left and right
flop apart, the sun pours down
and, winged, the dull heat is swarming
over me, through me, shushing
within in the throbbing red –
it mounts to my womb, as if
in half sleep I were to conceive
twins by two fathers, both
girls, one blond, one dark:
one of them aches and pulsates,
the other glisters and is not.

Evening

What is white outside
comes red through the rusty brown
the curtain's a shadow theatre
there are phosphorous pools on the armrest
There's mossy light on the carpet
it is woven into the pillow
But the glass is ice blue
a splintered resistance   Bars
of shadow split a burning
triangle into trapezoids
A shimmer of book spines
The hideous wallpaper fades
My room now is divided
into equal shadow halves
by a fluid wall of embers
Now from a dark armchair
I dip my foot in it
it flares I whip it back
it dies down   A thin flowing
hand gropes over our bed
slides over our cooling patch
It shapes the where-we-lay
from the folds in high relief
an objective memory un-
wrapped from our flagging morning
where still my shadow thighs
are clasping your shade hips

No longer

No longer shall I lay my heart open
or strive towards a goal.
This sober July, this sheer madness
that blooms by system and is organized,
burns in each sense as salt burns in a wound.
It is a southern moment: between walls,
beneath bright awnings, among evergreens,
its dark, holy statue stands –
a saint who with mouth caved in must be a hundred.
An ice-cold glance at the world cannot endure
its counterpart: blind face
turned to the moon, hair streaming in the wind:
ecstasy. What is the eye for, if all
its focus is the sky or the dim future?
What is fire for, fever or pale
obsession, thorn or flame?
And what is ultimate love for?
Why should I choose? Why, if it does not exist,
seek heavenly flame, that the winged form
might in time reveal itself from beneath the flesh?
Whatever substance bodily joy was once
made of, it ages ago burned out. Why
a unique hope, rather than ten thousand?
From the net which is our selves, there is no
getting disentangled, no way out, and no
solution: not by undoing the knot,
picking at it, pulling it even tighter,
or vanishing through your own interstices
in the waters of the world.

Summer solstice

It's August again and the sky is tinted
    a lustreless mother-of-pearl, shedding sunstrokes.
I see a sumac vegetating in the crevices
    of the tarred roof where it's grown.
A sunbathing woman on the pale grass of the beach
    goes dizzy, turbans her head with a towel
and, her cheek sucked in, investigates
    her face in a pocket mirror.

The melon's flesh is green glass, in the apricot's flesh
    there is someone's blood. On the road
candy-floss heat; everything, gone translucent,
    seems on the point of melting.
Ice-cream runs, cold pearly drops
    burn on your sweaty skin, your shirt sticks to you.

From the well of the dark courtyard the sounds
    of a TV film – the windows are all open.
I start, I've forgotten to draw the curtain –
    the screen of the night sky, left on,
blankly humming, shines grey on me.
    Last year's death appears, as ever
on a chair beyond my range of vision.
    In my dream a pale foot
is struggling its way up through muddy earth.

A gladiolus explodes in slow motion,
    it spreads from the bottom upwards:
it takes some days for the yellow or red
    flame to get to the top.
When day is done there's a white light
    behind my closed eyes: from the horizon
comes a shooting star that whirls, shudders, takes shape
    as a brooding bird of light that says to me 'my daughter'.

There are slow chandeliers being turned above our heads,
   the Lion, all aglow, moves into Virgo,
and all things thereafter will be changed.
Everything completed falls through a sieve, whatever
   has ripened comes to an end . . .
no, it won't, only now will all bear fruit,
   so have no fear now, have no fear, no fear.

Rakovszky: translated from the Hungarian by Clive Wilmer and George Gömöri.

TIBOR ZALÁN

Tibor Zalán was born in 1954 and studied Hungarian and Russian literature at the University of Szeged. His first poems were published in the mid-1970s; since then he has brought out five books of poetry, of which *Give Me Respite, Time!* is the most ambitious. Zalán absorbed the technical innovations of the Hungarian avant-garde of the twenties but lately has been edging closer to a more traditional attitude, trying to achieve a synthesis of modernism and tradition. His poems convey an obsessive absorption with his immediate surroundings.

'The wind the night the endless snowfall'

the wind the night the endless snowfall perhaps
these gothic things yet perhaps these
the moon the blinding black sun and the bloodstained
cloaks rustling in the depths of darkness – do you see
see how easily you slip from among the obediently
streaming words into nothingness. meanwhile the nights march
just march like sullen faceless soldiers
my nights slog between the walls swollen from fear
that which can be shown, cannot be said
between the swollen walls of my nights faceless sullen
soldiers slog from fear just marching the nights
march into nothingness. meanwhile from among streaming
words you obediently slip: well that's how easily
still how easily i write the poem – do you see
see streaming cloaks in the depths of the bloodstained
darkness and the sun the blinding black moon and perhaps
yes these gothic things perhaps these
the endless snowfall the night the wind

Translated from the Hungarian by Gerard Gorman.

'I haven't told you yet'

i haven't told you yet but while you're somewhere else laughing
i dream of murder: of your rolling head your
vulnerable skull drying on the mantel. the knife
cast into night resting in your body the axe
lowered into the dawn fracturing your shoulder. look my style
is killingly simple. i scrutinize myself in order to be lean
like these lines – unwritable. i scrutinize what can be
destroyed in my self. is any existing certainty destined for me
besides death – the undefeatable
now i dream of your murder
you can't mean more than a guilty conscience. you'll be
a blurred kite hovering above the city of dreams a
vague ship sunk into the dream water. like a plant
your body fluids will suck up my nerves bitter salt
you'll be bitter salt in the night hour. then suddenly you'll
cease to exist just like the hour and the ship
the kite won't be either. there'll be just darkness
a charred match behind the swinging doors of infinity

Translated from the Hungarian by Gerard Gorman.

'The women we write poems about'

the women we write poems about
we don't know. perhaps behind the mists
in the rising sun they turn their pale heads aside
perhaps scrutinizing us from behind
our bitter cigarette smoke
more callously than babes.
we seek their homes and they move in blazing clothes
over glowing fields yet all in vain. we summon them and
the ice barks upwards in our mouths
perhaps the soaked skulls of dreamers
guard their unbearable silence. perhaps in this white
lunacy their dizzy existence becomes clear
we write the poems they'll never read
about those who night after night by the moon sing
their sweatshirts upon us flying away above the trees
in light summer dress and who
in our poems droop into housewives mothers
lovers cringing in borrowed rags. upon their brows
death fastens. the fine copper bells fade in their
dancing breasts through the murkiness of our drinks we
see them still. their slender backs swinging hips leave us
in the red twilight to be with others now and forever
joyless

Translated from the Hungarian by Gerard Gorman.

'By dawn the shadows reach
the windowsill'

by dawn the shadows reach the windowsill. this
is my time when the silvery layers
stretch into infinity. listen
to my scream once at dawn: i am recognition
and fear together and all this is by chance no more:
in me is matter organized into reason. i meet
the moment of my death just when my birth still lives in me
listen how i shudder in this immense solitude
of self-recognition. listen so i'll have a living witness when
i awaken in the salty garment of my sweat
my shadow reaches over the earth –
at dawn i suffer the impossible – existence –
cuddled in the amniotic fluid of first morning light i float
slantwise in time. death too happens to me my salt-white thirst
keeps me turning among the crystal bars of light the bats
of my hair. by dawn shadows reach the windowsill. silver layers
stretching to infinity
spread apart at such a time
this is my time
the universe upholds me in its arms now. eternity
towers in the beams of my eyes.

Translated from the Hungarian by Daniel Hoffman.

IMRE ORAVECZ

Imre Oravecz questions with a voice that pits the elegiac against the existential. He was born in 1944 and lives in Budapest. Oravecz's first collection of poems, *Hey!*, came out in 1972. His most recent book, *September 1972*, was highly acclaimed when it appeared in 1988. One Hungarian reviewer described the collection as 'a series of sighs which build up into an articulate statement'. His voice preserves a defiant ambiguity, fusing confession with accusation, passion with purposelessness.

from *September 1972*

In the beginning
                    there was *you*, there was there, there was then, there was the blue sky, there was the sunlight, there was the spring, there was the warmth, there were the fields, there were the flowers, there were the trees, there was the grass, there were the birds, there was the forest, there was friendship, there was determination, there was grace, there was trust, there was the giving, there were the riches, there was the joy, there was the gaiety, there was laughter, there was song, there was speech, there was adulation, there was praise, there was respect, there was understanding, there was sweetness, there was purity, there was beauty, there was affirmation, there was faith, there was hope, there was love, there was the future, then you became she, there became here, then became now, the blue sky became black smoke, the sunlight rain, spring became winter, the warmth became cold, the fields became marshes, flowers became dry stalks, trees turned to ash, the grass to mud, the birds to quarry, strength to weakness, courage to cowardice, determination became indecision, grace became awkwardness, trust became suspicion, the giving became selfishness, the riches turned to poverty, the joy to sorrow, the gaiety to gloom, the laughter to

tears, the song to screaming, the speech to stammering, adulation became damnation, compliments became curses, respect became disdain, understanding became conflict, sweetness turned to bitterness, purity to filth, beauty became a toad, affirmation became negation, faith became doubt, hope became despair, love became hate, the future became the past, and the whole thing began all over again.

I remember clearly,

    the day you first came to me, short skirt, see-through blouse, light sandals, your baggage as light as a feather, somehow like you, sunny as the spring that brought you, wide awake, responsive to everything around you, and young, almost a child, in a child's body, downy and fresh, you told me every detail of your journey, pass control and customs, the scenery from the train, how people treated you, and how it felt to be in the *eastern bloc* for the first time, surprised by what to me was commonplace, and finding commonplace the things that surprised me, you liked the city, the old villas, the streets, the bridges, the pastry shops, the museums, the swimming-baths, the uniforms policemen wore, the trams, and you tried so hard in bed to make up for all you'd missed betimes, and always saw to it that I was pleased with everything, because you were pleased with everything, delighted in it all, in me, in yourself, in the world, and no less clearly when you last came to me, a long two-piece suit, a bulky sweater, walking shoes, your baggage heavier, and you too somehow heavier, overcast, like the autumn that brought you, withdrawn, already indifferent to certain things, and older, a woman, in a woman's body, mature and tired, no mention of pass control and customs, of the scenery from the train, of how they treated you, or of how it felt to be in the *eastern bloc* again, no longer surprised by what to me was commonplace, nor finding commonplace the things that surprised me, indifferent to the city, unmoved by the old villas, the streets, the bridges, the pastry shops, the museums, the swimming-baths, the uniforms policemen wore, the trams, and you no longer tried so hard in bed to make up for all you'd missed betimes, nor did you see to it that I was pleased with everything, for you were no longer pleased with everything, no longer delighted in it all, in me, in yourself, in the world.

I'm trying to imagine you now

                      not as the radiant young girl I knew, but as a dull middle-age woman I've never seen, your legs thick and your hips broad, but your waist still slim, you graduated from the university with honours, you're a researcher in a famous Scandinavian institute, your husband is Scandinavian, it was on his account you went to live abroad, he's a great scholar, a man of consequence, once he adored you, these days he neglects you, but within you a flame still burns for him, though not for the northern country where you're a foreigner and freeze both winter and summer, yet you stick it out with the help of frequent phonecalls home, pouring out your troubles to your mother, no, even the slimness of your waist is a thing of the past, and your once silky skin is disfigured by scarlet blotches, but your breasts have kept their former buoyancy, as a student you were not outstanding, and you're a simple surgeon in your new home, at a hospital in the capital where they only give you minor operations, you've grown distant from your husband, a worthy man with weak nerves, you often quarrel, you betray him, find refuge in your work, accept more night duty to spend less time under the same roof, and you constantly threaten him with divorce, but lack the courage to leave, no, your breasts begin to sag, and the sweet lines of your face have all turned bitter, but your gaze is still candid, you barely passed your exams, and you're a second-rate district doctor in the provinces, you prescribe the same three or four tablets for every complaint and refer every petty illness to a specialist, you've never loved your convivial, if untalented husband, but still you get along, you have a Ford Sierra, all to yourself, holidays by warm seas, dinner guests, rack your brains over recipes, vote for the People's Party, Mario Simmel is your favorite author, you adore TV films, drindl, curd-cheese strudel, and you want to live till you're a hundred, the candour of your gaze is in ruins . . . no, I cannot imagine you.

The sun is shining,
                    the snow sparkling, the air calm, the ever-
greens droop beneath their burden of whiteness, I walk the streets
of a deserted neighbourhood, the flats and the houses empty,
those who have work are at work, the children are at school, only
the elderly huddle behind drawn curtains, it's cold, I'm dressed
for the season, red cheeks, a shopping bag, milk, bread, pickles
from the local market, within my budget for the day, my dog
catches up with me, limping on three legs, frozen snow between
his nails, rolls over and nibbles at the irritating slippers, sees a cat
and chases after it, awkwardly a car backs out of a garage, the
engine revving loud, but disturbing no one, sparrows swarm
around a dustbin, pecking at the food among the rubbish, a
solitary blackbird on a telegraph wire observes with interest, I've
had breakfast and my organs function tolerably well, im-
perceptible metabolism, something destroyed, something restored,
air inhaled and released, through the nose because of the cold,
my birthday, my fortieth, never thought I'd live to see it, already
on my way out, can see the other shore, barren, stony, hostile,
never pictured it that way, but don't complain, I feel the passage
of time yet do not hurry, one step after another, keeping a steady
pace, taking the familiar route, I have time, no more grand plans
swirling in my head, the storms too have subsided, I only think of
the unavoidable, repetitive daily chores, surrender to them, peel
away at their significance, and I'm pure as the winter morning,
at peace and without care, almost free.

All I want

is what is still to come, the slow estrangement, the
terrible finale, the absolute defeat, personal, made to measure, my
very own, I want to stand and face it now, eye to eye, the defeat
I've always kept at bay, to live with it, in a cage, like living with a
wild animal, to feed it, nurture it, tame it, learn from it, until
finally I'm prepared to give up everything I've ever clung to, to
throw it all into the fire like so much worthless junk, then, as if
paralysed, I'll stop doing all the things I still go on doing, I'll even
give you up, and there will no longer be a past, or a present, nor
will there be a you, for I do not want a you, only the future,
beautiful, without mercy.

Oravecz: translated from the Hungarian by Richard Aczel.

POLAND

POLAND

RYSZARD KRYNICKI

Ryszard Krynicki is the key figure of the 'New Wave', the generation of '68, dedicated to portraying the ills inherent in communist Poland. He was born in 1943 in Sankt Valentin, Austria, and studied Polish literature at Poznań University. His close association with the dissident movement barred official publication since the mid-1970s, though *Our Life Grows* was published by Kultura in Paris in 1978 and circulated in *samizdat* in Poland. *Not Subject to Oblivion* was published in 1989 in two versions. A reticent individual, Krynicki's poems are sparse meditations on the periphery of prayer.

'How does it rise'

how does it rise from the fall? from falling
to the knees? weakened from fear or bent
in humility? from a broken sentence,
which gives us to mercy – or gives us mercy?
from trustful faith? or untrusting faithfulness?
how
and against whom,
against whom does it rise
against whom does it run, the poem? hope?

and the fear of fulfilment?

1967/1980

It, sleepless

It is I,
though hungry and sick,
who abandoned a home
left to hunger and sickness.

I am: no. Speechless,
long forgotten
wandering empty streets.

Night, one of many, the only one.
A shadow hidden
in someone's dark window
lashed by the cool glare of the moon.)

It hangs
on the cross.

(Forgive me.
And You, and You.)

1977, Vienna

'The beginning crossed out'

for Zbigniew Herbert

The beginning crossed out, on the other
side: whiteness.

so much life in between,
inexpressible –

and a sheet of paper: crumpled
burning in an ashtray

a small infinity? nothing?
morsel of light and shade

1974, 1985

Journey through death I

She combs her infinite, radiant hair
in front of a greying mirror
as if she were sleepless, racing through herself –
a strange body, burning in a dream,
lost
within the white blizzard of skin that surrounds,
imprisons and liberates

Mirror, reflection of nothingness, greying in horror –
the light of extinguished stars –
looks with her stranger's eyes
and the blind, clairvoyant moment remains
the mirror solely exists: out of the sucking emptiness
it emerges, expands
grows ever more precise – a polished surface
of glass
of metal

and she, twice dead in her separation,
quickly, as if she wanted to catch
the last tram,

combs her hair

Journey through death III

Perhaps you'll suddenly
leave your home.

Perhaps you'll awake in a strange body,
beyond the walls of an asylum with unknown victims
perhaps on a square
red from blood;

naked,
nameless
with a dead tongue,
mute heart;

Perhaps you won't awake
perhaps you won't return;

perhaps you'll meet Jan Palach,
your contemporary,
who burned helpless in the heart of Europe
protesting alone against foreign armies:
your vanquished country's army
among them;

perhaps you'll meet the workers from the coast
bearing stigmata
on their wounded foreheads;

perhaps you'll meet no one,
perhaps you'll meet no one,

perhaps you'll awake in me.

'How lucky it is'

How lucky it is: two survivors from Warsaw,
Betár, Drohobych ghetto,
we meet at the Central Station
built on ashes, breaths, the dust of the dead,
murdered, nameless, missing,
and we remember, silent, our dead,
murdered, nameless, missing without trace,
an immortal sky and dead landscapes,
freedom, equality, brotherhood and compassion,
alpha and omega of smoke buried shallow in the resettled air,
scraps of burned paper, ghosts of letters and books
soaring on vertical currents still higher, further,
transcending all inhuman, movable, poisonous borders,
shadows of burned books crumbling at the touch,
ghosts of our old and new, dead and living oppressors,

and we remember our old teachers
and girls who live only in our hearts
and the unending rattle of their shoes

beyond haunted windows.

Krynicki: translated from the Polish by Michael March and Jarosław Anders.

TOMASZ JASTRUN

Tomasz Jastrun was born in 1950 and lives in Warsaw. His first book of poems, *Without Excuse*, was published in the early 1970s. He worked with the underground publishing house NOWA and joined the Gdańsk shipyard workers during the 1980 August strikes. Later he worked for the Mazowsze Solidarity Region as an editor of their 'Cultural Bulletin'. When martial law was declared in 1981, Jastrun went into hiding. Arrested in November 1982, he was interned in Białołęka camp. Two volumes of poetry were brought out in *samizdat*: *At the Crossroads of Asia and Europe* and *White Meadow*. He is presently an editor at *Res Publica*, an independent journal. Though he would deny the charge, he is the finest poet of his generation.

The seed

Birds
Fly into the depths of our existence
Frightened
They fold and unfold
Their wings

Birds
Fly through the fading corridor

Dead tired
They rest on our shoulders
They are hungry

Our hands are already empty
The seed
Within our eyes and lips

Translated from the Polish by Michael March and Jaroslaw Anders.

The Polish knot

There was no good solution
Therefore it shrank and darkened
There was no good solution
Therefore uprisings broke out like sobs

There is no good solution
Therefore everyone wears
The Gordian Knot
On his neck

When you cut it
You cut the throat

Translated from the Polish by Michael March and Jarosław Anders.

Scrap

After us there will be
Neither scrap metal
Nor laughter
From start to finish
We held no illusions
All our uprisings
Lie packed in the hall
With a toothbrush
and a towel

When someone knocks on the door
The echo pounds
Through the solitary years
But there is no call to action
No convoy to Siberia
Only the upstairs neighbour whose sink
Once again has overflowed
Comes wringing his hands to warn us

Translated from the Polish by Daniel Bourne.

Hat

This elderly gentlemen
also takes walks in the Yard
But his hat clashes
with the barbed wire
and the bars muzzling the windows
as though they were afraid we might bite through
This man with a hat
is here because he sought
to overthrow the government by force
and violate our treaties.

Sixty years old
his hands furrowed like the earth
of pre-war Europe
and a very dangerous hat
on his head

Translated from the Polish by Daniel Bourne.

Nothing

I am forgetting him as though he walked
Who knows where
Through the streets of a strange city

Unexpectedly I find
My first home
With fragrant stairs
And wooden balustrade

Taking his book from the shelf
A bird flies out and rests
At the limits of my strength

Nearby a new housing estate is built
With concrete slabs
By people with frozen hands

And I feel my hair bristle with fear
For invariably in the face of death
What terrifies most is
That almost *nothing has happened*

Translated from the Polish by Michael March and Jarosław Anders.

Fruit

Even love
Can be torn away
Like dressing
Off the great wound of the face

Even that wound
Can be torn away

The scream remains

And even it
Can breed
Wild fruit

Our hungry children
Reach

Translated from the Polish by Michael March and Jarosław Anders

JAN POLKOWSKI

Jan Polkowski was born in 1953 and lives in Kraków. He studied Polish literature at Jagiellonian University and was active in the Student Solidarity Committee and Kraków Students' Press. In 1980 he was one of the co-founders and editors of ABC, an independent publishing house. In 1981 he worked for the Małopolska Solidarity Region. Polkowski was arrested and interned on 13 December 1981. Underground publishers brought out three collections of his poetry. In 1986 Puls in London published *Poems 1977–84*. Polkowski's poems have a tough, urban staccato, an 'indestructible blade which cuts you into good and evil'.

'The world is only air'

The world is only air
shining, granular, transparent things,
fleeting breath, through which I see
time.

Thought is more material
(footprints in the snow, the smell
of crushed grass, a leaf caged
in the fist of the wind).

The silent word is more
palpable
than wood, wall, flesh – invisible
proof of Eden.

I don't know that man

I clearly hear the crowing of a rooster,
I have not misheard,
crowing in the middle of a concrete garden,
though invisible to sight.
I write it down, I freeze, I listen,
but someone writes with my hand:
'Haven't you renounced me, Galilean?'
(Are you afraid?)

Bleeding breast

A nursing woman. Birds (Are you
hungry?)
A grey shoal, city, carriages of air
soaring. (Eat, earth.)
Half a loaf for me, half for you,
deadly wings.

Noli me tangere

Gesture of an Ionic column returning your face
gesture of slender fire returning you, page by page,
the book of generations,
oval of a marble breast, the oval of a pregnant womb
    of an imprisoned woman
bestowing upon you the stony alphabet of humanity
the untouchable whiteness of a hostage's shirt (Goya, *The
Third of May 1808*) dressing the world in fountains of colour,
dark chant of a psalmist,
damp taste of a couplet – indestructible blade which cuts you
into good and evil.

Tell me

What does it mean, you stand in front of me
and cry

Smash that stone – inside there is
a face.

You don't talk to me, because you are capable
of love.

A tree and a stone feed you
like an infant.

Forgive me, God, send out
the pigeons.

You cry as only forgetting
cries.

Limitless mirrors, uncertain
death.

Dusk

October, Miles Davis – *Lonely Fire*,
gentle haze, loving and warm.
Did we experience much?
Probably not, since we no longer expect anything.

On this day of yellowing chestnut trees, darkening ash trees,
under a painful sun: slave-poets will continue to claim,
they are not political activists,
political prisoners – unwilling to be slaves,
murderers – that they are sent by Providence.

Close your eyes.
(We'll touch our hands, a bright gesture of ash.)

Those cursed words
are only lines from your song, only searching for
perfect darkness (lonely
fire).

Polkowski: translated from the Polish by Michael March and Jarosław Anders.

BRONISŁAW MAJ

Bronisław Maj was born in 1953 in Łódź. He studied Polish language and literature at the Jagiellonian University in Kraków and co-edited the influential magazine *Student*. He worked as a scriptwriter and actor in the KTO Theatre. Under martial law Maj circumvented censorship by running in Kraków a popular spoken literary monthly, *Speaking Out*, which was awarded an honorary prize by Solidarity in 1984. The magazine is now continuing under Maj's editorship in printed form. Maj has published five collections of poems. A selection, *Destruction of the Holy City*, was published in London by Puls in 1986.

'The silence in a house'

The silence in a house where someone
is dying: whispers, handkerchief-stifled sobbing, gently
closing doors. The smell of medicines no longer
needed, the yellow Candlemas candle-flame. That
silent man, my father, is a boy
whose mother is dying. No one yet believes
in what is now happening, has
already happened, unnoticed, but still
this silence. Someone's beating a carpet in the courtyard,
a car starts up, a quarrel on the stairs,
music, a grass-scented draught
has snuffed out the candle. Nothing here
belongs to her any more. We have nothing
in common with her any more, we remain behind.
Now we can weep loudly, louder:
in constant witness
to life.

'In the forest at night'

In the forest at night a fire: a wavy circle
of light, beyond it there is nothing
because we are here, in the middle:
rousing cries, songs, laughter . . .
Now the firewood is all gone, the flames
expire. And we also say: man
expires. And there is still something of fire
there. Then nothing: darkness and we see clearly all
that's remained: our faces suddenly all so
different, bent over this place, black
outlines of trees, somewhat brighter sky,
cold stars. And no one knows why
we remain silent so long
and then talk
in whispers.

'Seen fleetingly'

Seen fleetingly, from a train:
a misty evening, grey streaks of smoke
hanging motionless over a field,
the wet blackness of earth, the sun almost
set – against its fading disc, afar,
two tiny specks: women in dark shawls,
perhaps returning from church, perhaps
one is talking, some ordinary tale,
perhaps of sinful love – her words
distinct and simple, but they could serve
to create everything from the beginning.
Remember this, for ever:
the sun, ploughed earth, women,
love, evening, these few words
good for a start, remember –
perhaps by tomorrow we shall be
somewhere else

'Evening at Kraków Central Station'

Evening at Kraków Central Station: three tiny
gypsy beggars: with the unconscious charm of nimble cheerful
    little animals
they scurry through the crowd, vanish, call out in an
    incomprehensible tongue.
You have nothing in common with them, only, momentarily, the
    warmth
of the coin, which – quickly, shame-faced – you press into the
    little hand
of a proud and self-confident four-year-old; her condescending
    smile, a glance
older than you, than memory: a dizzy apprehension of another
reality. Now she runs away, you see a bobbing plait, a kerchief,
bare soles: she feels the cold marble of the stairs differently,
    she sees differently
a crowd of people like you, she hears but doesn't understand
    the loudspeaker
announcements and doesn't realize how free she is, doesn't
    realize
how she is breathing: how lightly she cancels and rejects
your world. Later, in a corner, the three noisily divide
the spoils; the eldest shouts – they run away. You remain
and then suddenly, a breath-taking desire: to be
one of them: to feel dampness and chill powerfully with bare
    feet,
scurry briefly through this poor alien world and return, now:
now! urging your own in an unknown tongue, running,
happy like a child
of an unknown
God.

'A leaf'

A leaf, one of the last, broke off a maple branch,
it swirls in clear October air, falls
on a pile of other leaves, grows dark and still. No one
admired its rousing battle with the wind,
no one followed its flight, no one will distinguish it now
lying among other leaves, no one had seen
what I had, no one. I am
alone.

Maj: translated from the Polish by Adam Czerniawski.

EAST GERMANY

WOLFGANG HILBIG

Wolfgang Hilbig sees through 'the glass of drowned mirrors'. His work disperses the ego to the far corners of time. Dichotomy becomes reality, fathering in darkness phantoms of love and death. Born in 1941, he began his life as a miner's son. In 1979 he published his first volume of poems after various jobs in the construction trade. He continued writing in Leipzig, though much of his work remains unpublished in East Germany.

The names

1

written in thunderstorm light
and dream
        in half-darkness the
barely discernible words unchain themselves
strive to get out into the wet like
rain to transform the earth

I speak of great peace: outside
it is cold wasted empty outside
the tumult
        but the words want their names:
to move the housing estates from their foundations
the sea to disregard warnings and storm
the shores

the names assume shapes horrible
bearded gods howling for fire
and sword they throw me on the bed
and cut open my skull

2

rain slivered light
rose neon streaks attack the street
the land boundaries of my generation
dissolve
                marked in blood
castration urine *ach* surrendering
I inscribe the names in washed-out
gaps in the script

love joy confusion; names of sand
sifted from bodies of paving stones
panic tumult: potted plants in anger
throw their stalks at the window pane

and I can talk
can talk until I'm drenched
                                in vain swear:
my words must remain here . . .
finally I see the rain founder
outside on your rotted
wall leonardo

'You have built me a house'

you have built me a house
let me begin another

you have placed a chair for me
now put dolls in your lounge chair

you have saved money for me
I would rather steal

you have opened a road for me
I'll slash my way
through shrubs at the side of the road

should you say
go alone
I would go
with you

Absence

how much longer will our absence be endured
no one notices the black that shapes us
how we have crawled into ourselves
into our blackness

no we shall not be missed
we have strong broken hands stiff necks –
this pride of things destroyed and dead
look at us – bored-to-death things – there
has never been such destruction

and we shall not be missed our words are
frozen scraps fallen in light snow
where trees glitter white in frost – yes
and waiting to fall

all has been destroyed – at the end
our hands broken our words broken: come
go away stay here – a restless speech
confused and indifferent
which we follow beside our absence

follow the way in the evening
as stray dogs follow us with sick
uncomprehending eyes

Awareness

in the name of my skin
in the name of my craft
in the name of this country
where care carelessly feeds
in the name of that torn
name that lovers
secretly whisper to each other
in the name of these forbidden
pains
    to dress
confusion in words
                I've taken
this screaming office
                  unto myself

Entrance

silt
from the moon between us. gold
in the sky. and I'm to be purified unto blood
shaved cold to the skeleton beneath star-kissed
trees rotting in the marshes. where I'm to be
transmuted into the negative of a rendezvous: o waiting
what a wretched career . . .
dreadful bourgeoisie that will not admit me
which I've betrayed for your sake
                                        you love
my bone universe that stands opposed to reality
which stole away proof of my existence.
away . . . for existence remains a print
which darkness defiles to prevent our falling
into the hole of irredeemable purity . . .
away from this well-lit hole
towards which I once crawled without joy or anger
submissively transformed into reality
in which I was to be no more than this: locus

Hilbig: translated from the German by Agnes Stein.

LUTZ RATHENOW

Lutz Rathenow has clashed with the authorities for years. He was born in 1952 in Jena. After finishing his studies and his term in the army he found a job as a transport worker. In 1977 he moved to East Berlin to write unproduced plays for the theatre. Forbidden to travel abroad and unwilling to leave, he adopted a photocopying machine to earn his living. *Forceps Delivery* was published in 1987 and *Tenderly the Fist Revolves* a year later. While Rathenow's poetry has a strong activist direction, it is often derived from the world of dream.

More notes on the theme of changing places

For example changing streets.
Famous memorials.
Places.
Or whole cities. Major cities.
An exchange of people worth thinking about.
Or, because simpler to realize, a change of administrations.
Every administration to rule for a certain length of time
every country on this earth.
Taking turns, so that the leader of San Marino rules the
    USA
at the same time as the leader of the USA rules San
    Marino.
Completely new dimensions in understanding peoples seem
possible. Of course institutions in the service of power to
move from country to country. To avoid complications, first
of all armed services.
And of course never parallel to the country of origin.
So that possibly for two months China will have a
Japanese police, the Soviet Army an American secret service

and a state administration from the DDR.

If this sounds too confusing it might be better to exchange systems right away.

The planetary system.

Cosmic exchange of place has had little practice, while on earth individuals accomplish the most astonishing exchanges.

Somebody working in one state suddenly appears as trusted confidante in another threatened state.

In any case a visible motion is not necessary to effect a change of residence. Many Germans managed it without making a move in 1933 and 1945.

Finally, as a last possibility of making a change, one could renovate. Which is how many talk themselves into thinking something new has been effected.

Dreams

Always there is a city
a crumbling wall
and faces of friends
always changing

Always stars
tracer shells
you seek to escape

And an anxious fear
driving you from place to place
to hide something
which you nevertheless lose

Which then saves you
just as they're about to seize you

Prague

Why now the visit
middle of winter, in this city
so long joined to frost.

Hurriedly everybody empties his mouth
of sentences and flees the streets
for a warmer place.
A coffee in the café, the wait
for a friend who never arrives.
Talk with two strangers.
In a book Jiri Walkers will read:
*Racked with pain I broke
your pair of eyes to pieces.*
Someone wraps a face in a scarf,
the scratching noise of a needle
on a never-ending record.

Why right now a poem
middle of winter, on this city,
which I haven't visited for years.

To the poet Franz Kafka

Stay in your small room. Keep watch
at posts long lost. There, where no one
any longer suspects an enemy – where scorn
and medals are assured you. Keep watch
with your hope your misgivings of losing your head
to this terror. Give us news
of the talk of things, the battle
in us: those silent battles
we pass over not noticing. Hold fast
in your large room – let the small world
wind up: Facing the eye in the word
use the whip, drive it to bursting
on the helpless helpful paper. Give us news
of all screams which we do not hear
all the murders to which we're accustomed.
Remain strong in your weakness
permit the word its enormous power: To be honest
in its impotence, glorify nothing
of its impotence. Remain in your room
join us in future battles: Give us courage
with your fear

Faith

1

As a child I sometimes
wanted to pray
simply to crush
doubt
between folded hands

2

Later the wait.
For a God.
In order to kill him.
With reverence.

Rathenow: translated from the German by Agnes Stein.

STEFFEN MENSCHING

Steffen Mensching was born in 1958 in East Berlin. He studied aesthetic and cultural theory at Humboldt University and worked as an actor with a free theatre group and as an editor for the literary magazine *Temperamente*. His second collection of poems, *Feel of the Cloth*, was published in 1986. There is in his work 'a gesture of human closeness, a touching search for contact, drawing near to material that protects, secures, warms and hides'.

For Peter Weiss

Some time, later,
we shall break the archive seals.
Sitting together then
we shall utter what has never been said before.

On the table lay hands
no longer balled into fists.
No movement of fingers.
No one to fall on any one.

Betrayed sacrifices traitors
      trials hearings depositions charges

Some time, hopefully soon, but later,
we shall bear the whole truth.

We shall name heroic heroes
     wrong the wrong

one after another we shall announce ourselves in words
break the silence.

The light will be bright those days
when we show each other our wounds
our blows caused each other,

the old suppurating scars, the cursed
          the odious
into which our enemies groped
with dirty sweaty hands
          to shame our dead.

We would not diminish victory
          only make it cleaner

Translated from the German by Agnes Stein.

'My coal merchant drives a Tatra'

My coal merchant drives a Tatra
Black as coal he rolls past me. Sometimes
I want to wave to him
With a tiny little flag. I learned that as a child.
But he would misunderstand it,
Possibly. And then who knows how harsh
Winter might get in the days to come.

Translated from the German by Margitt Lehbert.

'Your hair was drenched'

Your hair was drenched
In sleep, a black river
In a snowy landscape,
My lips rested on yours, you
Woke up, I went to war,
Said the man on the radio, I
Went lightly, pulling the blanket over us.

Translated from the German by Margitt Lehbert.

Dreamlike excursion with Rosa L.

Gone are we, all of a sudden, for a love
From the wreaths and marches of winter,
Out of the loud-hard streets of the city
Into the middle of a Polish wheat field.
And you, my friend, are so entirely different
Than I thought you'd be.
You throw your shoes, those sturdy ones,
Lightly into the stinking river.
I throw your picture in too and see you
Standing barefoot in the poppies. – They're red as the flag –
I call out, to please you, to the sky,
which lies grey, like my gaze, when you ask:
– Do people still, then, have no other eyes,
Child's mouth, evening glow, strawberries? –
I quickly gather a wreath of wheat into your hair,
Not a forgetful laurel on your grave.
And the earth, our clothes, our skin, are dry.
Only the birds take fright and scatter.
– *My innermost self* – you say – *belongs more to my sparrows*
than to my comrades. – At that my jaw drops
To my chest. – Now don't go right off smelling treason.
I'm sure I'll die *on my post*
In a street battle or in prison. –
And the hand that silences you
Are my lips, we hit the ground
Like wheat plunging in the wind.
Only somewhere sirens and shots bark out,
And already you're running away
Limping and naked, and I call out a greeting
And I'm afraid you'll die, and I'm afraid
You'll live and I jump up, and my foot
Gets caught in the marble, bows and lilies.

Translated from the German by Margitt Lehbert.

Jerry Mosololi [26] Simon Mogoerane [24] Marcus Motaung [28]

I had already forgotten you. One week after
    the execution.
When I emptied the rubbish you looked up at me
From the old newspaper. Dark doubting eyes.
    From the mould,
From the filth. How quickly, no-man's-land,
I thought. Forgiveness, I thought. Shit,
      I said sadly.

Translated from the German by Margitt Lehbert.

'In a hotel room in Meissen I read'

In a hotel room in Meissen I read
Not a line of Cleophon, a Greek
Epic poet, remains, no date.
Only that sliver of fame,
to be mentioned twice in the *Poetics*
of Aristotle. *He places*
Ordinary people before us. Drenched in sweat
I see him bending
A hexameter. *Language is clearest*
When it's made of common words.
And what else do I want. *But it appears flat*.
Says Aristotle. *An example*
Is the poetry of Cleophon. And if
He ever suspected it, I think
And slowly lower my ballpoint
On to the white sheet of paper.

Translated from the German by Margitt Lehbert.

KURT DRAWERT

Kurt Drawert was born in 1956 and lives in Leipzig. He has written for the theatre and worked as a translator. *Time Inventor* appeared in 1987 and *Personal Property* in 1989. He received the prestigious Lenz-Leona Prize for poetry in the same year. Drawert's poems gravitate between the sexes, exposing the optical illusions of everyday life.

Mirror symmetry

Enlarge the eyes, minimize
the nose, shorten the neck.

Displace, elongate, shift
ears, neck, head.

Lift the chin upwards
contract the brow. Curve

the mouth, round it, stretch
the skin, for the sake of harmony

change everything: like a poem
or the basic principles of life.

Translated from the German by Agnes Stein.

Clearing up

Take the old, decrepit, long
since used up, dirty dusty
things
away. Scrap the bed
on which one once lay,
burn the photographs, yellowed
and fingered, which reveal a former face.
: That, is supposed, to have been me? : Away!
Away with the letters
which bear witness
of those hours days years
in which one must have lived once already.
                              Away
with the joys and pains
of an existence experienced x times already
                              as a stranger
who walks through a stone age.
: Therefore destroy
what multiplies so quickly
and is recognized as signs :
things
through which we have become
our own guests
and which, every day anew,
betray us.

Translated from the German by Margitt Lehbert.

Simple sentence

for Dietrich Gnüchtel

Thoroughly the images
destroy themselves
and I am tired
of following them
as though they were a woman
who is the time
between May and September
in which the year
is still lacking a concept
for the colour
which slowly breaks down
from the wood of a park bench
empty and cold
above the snow.

Translated from the German by Margitt Lehbert.

For Frank O'Hara

Perhaps I will succeed
after all in writing a poem

in which no policeman
promenades through the

stanzas with austere
glances and red chalk.

An opportunity comes,
lies on the couch and

begins to open up.
To love it remains

easy as long as
grammar stands in the closet,

a book which cuts
up emotions into black

meaningless pieces that a
winter day blocks with drifts.

Translated from the German by Margitt Lehbert.

Defence

O how you speak, in your dreams, in the nights,
In the long, in the cold nights./ I listened
To your wishes, those hostile transmissions
Of consciousness, hear the repudiated words of day,
How they came and went as civil servants of sleep.
And your body, which bent round, rose and fell
And rose and fell, in the night,
In the long, in the cold night./ I sensed
Myself, steep, in the bed covers' hollow space and thought
Of a red, opening fruit which
Closes anew with the morning./ Then,
The next day, I disclosed your dreams to you
The way a denouncer reads statements from the record
Suitable for the charge./ I tried
Once more to lay my hand on yours,
Which, ready for defence, rose and fell
And rose and fell, on that day
On that bright, that short day.

Translated from the German by Margitt Lehbert.

ROMANIA

IOANA CRĂCIUNESCU

Ioana Crăciunescu is an actress by profession, working in cabaret, theatre and film. She was born in 1950 in Bucharest. A prolific poet, she was awarded the Writers' Union Prize in 1981. Her poems profess 'a boredom with history'. Her love poems are mythic nets – taut with the hunter, father, lover.

Shipwreck

I was in a field of potatoes
   peasants with hoes were tearing up
   the sail of my ship . . .

Those constantly buzzing flies
   were creating for me a world
   of bones and skin . . .

I was in a field of potatoes
   peasants were raking and gathering
   into stacks the ropes and helm,
   poop and prow of my ship;
   I smelt of potatoes,
   the shipwreck seemed
   an error of always navigating by the stars . . .

Red ants were running through my hair
thriftily
taking and carrying to their ant-hills
the wind and the frost, the taste and the scent,
the air, the salt of the sea . . .

I was in a field of potatoes
the peasants were mowing down the fixed masts
the earth smelt of earth again.
Farmer, load my ship, my life
on to wagons and cart it from the field . . .

Abundance in suffering

Without heads, without guts, with hearts beating
on a rubbish heap, each one
peeling off its skin in tubs of salt,
the eels are still thrashing about.

The tear sniffs out the eye.

The eye is the water in which I see them swimming,
twisting about, eels turning the grass
blood-red.

Knives are an extension of our caresses;
love is a remembering of this butchery.

City without a biography

In this city
the mute make declarations of love to each other
in different words.

In shop windows
on Persian carpets, faded women
learn Persian.

Under gas masks we hold in our teeth
wallets of papers
(the photo of mud-brick houses
in the fog).

Over my body runs an otter – your mouth
lost in the night.

Chronicle III

I made love with him in a hallucinative cave of darkness
on a floor of cinders, black maize at the edges,
my soul white.
At our heads bare white-washed gates stood guard; we could see
nothing but boundaries and deserted benches,
could hear nothing cleaving the air but the barking
of a starving pack of stray dogs.

I made love with him (he's just called 'him') on a sofa
dumped in an attic full of junk.
We heard nothing but creaking springs and falling straw,
saw nothing but blackened beams, the damp ceiling,
discarded portraits of dead kings; our muscles weakened,
our sweat smelt of the end of empire.

I made love with him at the Registrar's Office
and then at the lawcourts . . . We shared out between us
a few books, rhymes, a little love, ideas; black seconds
under the typewriter ribbon.

You sit on the same side of the road.
Like me you wear an armband.
You ask the same number of questions.

Her little red ear

Unspeakably beautiful heat. Her tapered
thigh shining in the swollen sun.

I looked at myself, beginning at my shoelaces.

Far away the dolphins were demonstrating
to small, darting fishes the elegance
of large gestures, the laziness of broad tolerance.

All the same,
I have confused her enough with my indifference!
I want to hear her moans,
to crowd her into corners and see her cracked
lips, to gaze into her eyes (she'll have
all those – eyes, nose, throat . . .?)

to hiss in her little red ear:

I adore you, I adore you; draw up my accounts!

A thousand and one nights

She wept with the son imprisoned in her belly.
Her skin was flowered with the king's bite marks,
the walls of her heart upholstered with ice.

The viper.

She made love with the deaf-mute manservants, then
played backgammon with the executioner – lost
camel after camel, whole caravans.

She slept covered in large fragments of mirror;
from her slow breathing the sun flowed down;
the planet rolled over lips cracked by the heat.

The viper.

She had loved: she smothered the air with that
well-embalmed sentiment.

Above the mountains of her country, the stars were lined up.

Crăciunescu: translated from the Romanian by Fleur Adcock.

ION MORAR

Ion Morar was born in 1956 in Şăiteni. He studied Romanian language and literature at Timisoara University and presently works as a journalist for the Bucharest student papers *Student Life* – renamed the *Word* after the revolution – and *Amphitheatre*. In 1987 *Indian Summer* was awarded the Début Prize of the Writers' Union; *The Smoke and the Sword* appeared in 1989. Morar recapitulates the entire poetical 'matter' of the Eighties generation.

The Trojan wave

to Virgil Mazilescu

Only excessive zeal caused the decline of great empires
time loading all virtues, all prophecies
on to a single ship.
I raise my hands, I raise my hands,
flags of flesh waving in an unknown language.
Only excessive zeal,
only you, distant on a single ship
enough for my poems to go blind,
to become my blindness, my amphora of carbonized
grain for the winter of the year one thousand
spent in a palace in Ephesus,
in Rome, in Alexandria, in Jerusalem.
(oh, I know: great cities are not built. They are born)
The ocean drives ashore not only the prejudices of history.
Anxious, I wait under Europe's sun
and social waves break on the rocks,
diseases file on in the limited spectrum of illusion
(I am healed, you are healed, he dies)

'In the evening we'll build a fire of seaweed on the shore

to dry ourselves, to keep the beasts at bay, *to found a family*.
We'd better not go back to the tribe.'
(If we add ourselves, we are three, if we subtract ourselves
you are only one)

He will embalm our feet.
(I am healed, you are healed)

One winter, one single day

Winter arrived for **one single** day like wet sheets
on the red retina of pain.
(you, loaded with electricity, leisurely leave the bed,
I shave but as if I were shaving the face of some savage,
my naked hands fumble through centuries. Not a single cut)
Winter arrived for a single day at the tent door
like a blinded animal; oh, tribe of mine, the day has come
for us to retire in furs (I can hear the voice of history in
        faraway slave markets)
I see and describe, see and describe.
My eager hands rush to the bread,
rush to your sparkling hair,
to the rotten apple.
Everything is in order.
Out of the small prophecies swarm insects,
out of the big ones pounce the tiger and the leopard.
I see and describe.
My eager hands rush to the bread, no, to your sparkling
hair, no, no, to the rotten apple.
One winter seen through the window of the classroom, the
        airport,
the barber's shop, the hospital. Nothing alarming,
nothing to warn you how the frail muscle of the heart will snap,
how madness will work havoc in the tribe,
how blood will fill the city.
Everything is in order. How many of us can look inside
and say, 'My soul is a happy book, a clean cup?'
Oh, tribe of mine, the day has come for us to retire in furs.
Night falls suddenly. For a while the rotten apple still glows

Salt wins

Ever smaller grows the flame by which I write,
ever greater: my age, dangers, the taste of earth in my mouth.
I can no longer describe myself. Salt wins, the ivy wins that
        scarcely
in a thousand years could bring down a house (the room where I
        sit
alone now, straining my hearing to the quick blood, trying to get
        carried away
by the rumbling of my cells as they construct my body. I can no
        longer describe myself).
I can no longer describe myself, though I know: they will scare
        you and run away,
they will scare me and be blinded.
Oh, what a heavy padlock my heart is on the door
between body and soul.
Pride will rise and say, 'Let me play with them for a little while
        still,
let me build up another empire.'
Salt wins, the bloodstain wins that's filled the library
(a few wild fruits on the work table)
I can no longer describe myself, I can no longer prophesy.
A bit of politics would cheer us up: salt does not win.
I stand among my years as in the most useful of exiles
'My life . . . ha-ha-ha! my plans . . . ha-ha-ha!'
I think by now my heart has grown another eye, already blind
'Alone we'll no longer manage to feed the bloodstain in the
        library,
we will no longer describe you,' say my poems.
But to love one another I must invent an incandescent language,
a few wild fruits ('let me play with them for a little while still')

And death indulges in a bit of rhetoric: a taste of earth

Standard isolation

I have been blind, blind as a mole
and I said to myself, 'I'll burn all the books
in the vulgar fire of doubt, I'll feed on sweet roots,
I'll sleep with my head on a stone'
Blind as a mole by a small heap of words.
The laws cut off the germinal bulbs of error,
pump the water into endless galleries.
'blind as a fruit'
Who will invent a language just to be alone?
'blind as a fruit, blind as a mole'
(Enthusiastic and illiterate, I loved you in African forests,
I fought with the missionary, sang late into the night,
'Eros kynegethikos, Eros kynegethikos,'
broke my poisoned arrows.
Then I took the books and burned them.)
But what do I see now? What can I describe when
eyes have sprouted all over my body?
An earth worm digs small, irregular galleries under my feet,
pain pushes me to the ocean, anaesthesia, mother,
I go into the water, I have burned all the books,
I grow transparent, transparent.
I see my heart within me: a happy red mole

The marquise went out at five o'clock

'give Marcel a madeleine to
calm him down,' says Madame Proust, and her son
writes books in the mirror, reversed, you will read them
facing the past, you advance backwards
until you hit the mirror, turn around, and see yourself
considerably aged and the one that you see cannot
suffer, the image follows you closely but
suffering is a ditch beyond which
this mirror's life unfolds,
from now on you have a paper past,
a madeleine that moulds suddenly
in an expectation whose end Marcel
continues to pull, 'rap his knuckles,
he's dipping the madeleine in ink,'
Madame Proust says, and her son
writes this very poem in the mirror
and while you've been reading it you've inevitably
aged: The marquise went out at five o'clock

Morar: translated from the Romanian by Oana Lungescu.

LIVIU IOAN STOICIU

Liviu Ioan Stoiciu was born in 1950 in Neamț county, Moldavia. He spent his childhood in a railway guard's cabin, which became the mythical setting of his first book of poems, *At the Railway Flag*. Unlike most of the poets of the Eighties generation, he left school for a variety of jobs: driver of mine wagons, waiter, archive keeper. In the autumn of 1989 Stoiciu sent an open letter to the president of the Writers' Union calling for the creation of a free writers' union. Stoiciu's poems are a delirium of evocation, a shorthand obsessed 'with the void, with death, with the confusion of things and the secret relationship between them'. *A Parallel World* was published in 1989.

'Archaic mothers'

archaic mothers, with belladonna
in their bosoms, coming down
on the waters of loneliness, With primrose milk
from the rolling field
in mind . . . Stem

broken from childhood, stream
out of which the soul of the dead man tried to grasp my
hand again today: good fragrance,
on a walk with you
in the middle of nature . . .
So many things and creatures
left behind: too
fleeting, impossible to capture on a photograph, unreal.
Creatures lost on the horizon ahead: who's that

looking for his shadow? No answer. At my

age, at noon, my back muscles
weakened, with a hazel wand, about to
discover a
treasure: excited, ready to take back what
has already assumed, in the earth,
in the grave, a shape of silver . . .

'From behind only the ashes'

from behind only the ashes settle calmly down, fail
to follow: that I am
all fragrance, at an age when
I watch myself in the mirror with a tolerant smile,
is no problem. Embodied
in what is most humble. An acacia
in bloom? Set out on a long road. Lacking

in any arrogance: and yet . . . how shall
I put it, for some time I've felt
the presence of a second being in me! Although I feel so alone.
'No, old man, it's only a moth:
busy pollinating. A hairy
moth?' No
moth, just look at the sores from the rope. I can feel

the presence of a second being in me. A young being,
younger, would you believe it and more nonchalant, unlike
me, ironical and shaped
at the mouth of the river. A primitive clay statuette . . .
River of the souls of our souls, beaten
with a quince rod, swollen,
ready to wash
the sacrilege away . . . Who is it? A newer
being? I watch myself in the mirror with a tolerant smile. It

anticipated me in everything: with
sardonic disdain for what I think is
deep in
me.

'In windy twilight'

in windy twilight, in the countryside. Where I haven't
slept since
childhood. Estranged, alone. From the
window hung
with quinces tasted by midges I watch the rope
for hanging pots
in the backyard: it looks restless. A
restlessness of the past? They say
at night empty pots are filled with the souls
of the dead and
move about until
they spill: here,
where the length of a man's shadow is laid
at the foundation
of the parental home. That's nothing

new, I'll
fill a pot myself: at the raven's
well. When –
ever. I'll fill it up: to the brim, how good, and
will I spill
into the village
brook? Bells are ringing
in the village: can you
concentrate on this for the moment? The brook
flows into the stream, in windy twilight, fish will
fly from branch to branch. The stream
in the air flows into the river,
the river . . . And
the sea, imagining
of my soul, Defeating

the force
of darkness: only a sound of broken pots, at the back

of my mind, faint,
heard every time I, masked,
get into bed and
I'm scared by all those that
suddenly appear, masked, excited, all my folk, father,
mother, grandmothers, grandfathers, great-grandfathers,
great-grandmothers, unicellular
organisms blown by the wind, yellow,
through the open window.

From the tower watching

Where the ashes of the day turn into
birds of multifarious colours . . . Ritual
birds. Every
hour? When obscure
forces, fluids and
dawnings
are suddenly revealed: there,
in distress
in the course of history:
family heirlooms. And how? Two
jokers were somersaulting towards what they had been. Day
and night: you
and I? They were two jokers
and we are like them: a contest in the tunnel. Now,
on the way back, walking on our hands. With

transparent hands, fossil
animals, driven away by the wave of primeval oblivion. Who
came first? Nostrils catching a forest
breeze, hair
touching the matter
that dissolves into rays . . . With
banners and bells. Old-
fashioned, standing up
to watch time
racing by.

Resurrection

I have just one measure for your unparalleled
solitude, my love: my unparalleled solitude. My love,
you are not of terrestrial origin. Out there,

in the moonlight, on
the banks of the
moaning river,
from the mammoth era, huddling together,
transformed for a minute into
each of the things you came across 'that you
like': through
these transformations
the world here has suffered great
losses. Has it indeed? It wasn't
us . . . We wanted to disturb nothing:
but our souls,
overflowing into the air, unruly . . . It was only
them: recovering
here the freshness
of their first
springs . . .

Where space changes its meaning

A pot of fired clay: around it
white clouds
are floating. A pot of fired clay, with
the outlines of lunar seas traced on the outside. A
pot where the souls of
the ancestors dwell: on the threshold, ready to fly
whenever we do. We, advocates of the
instantaneous
instauration
of melancholy. Can
we be regarded with hate? Yes, we can. We can
be hurt, made
prisoners: are you
foreign gods? Foreign gods. We, leaning forward
to embrace it, kiss it, drink
from it: a merciless
pot. A pot, a

green hill with a stream: repeat after me. Say it,
hand on heart, before you assuage
your thirst: here, I give
myself, I give
my town, my land, the water
flowing on it, my blood and
my soul and everything in my home,
I give all things that
belong to the gods.

A pot of fired clay. With each second
you recover who knows what epoch above
its rim: you call out
'comforting
forgetfulness' and it answers
in kind, a sweet echo . . .

Stoiciu: translated from the Romanian by Oana Lungescu.

ELENA ȘTEFOI

Elena Ștefoi writes 'as if the act of writing had become an inexplicable inner torture'. She was born in 1954 in Suceava county. Her poems have a 'tough, cutting structure, derived form her efforts to build on an alternative syntax, set apart by a sarcastic tension of extreme harshness'. Ștefoi's aggressive style, typical of the voice of the Eighties generation, must be seen as the poet's only weapon and defence against the alienation and fear pervading Romanian society. *Sketches and Stories* was published in 1989.

Love letter

What should you understand? A biography
that hangs on my words like
a ton of dynamite?
I know: I don't breathe by the rules,
my shoulders are slightly bent forward.
From noun to verb a murderous device
performs exercises in style
and waits for you.
Hear me out: I have lied,
stolen, betrayed my friends
shamelessly; I have stealthily
swallowed crumbs
from the tables of those
I despised.
I yearn for a clear ocean:
in which I could see, as I swim,
the future of vertebrae, within reach
of my sluttish understanding.
As often as you want,
you can count
these mistakes, passing like a head-waiter
between clients
at the height of the season.

Very close to the horizon

Once again
the next hour stumbles
and I can do nothing
to help.
It turns up at modest intervals,
looking like
the alcoholics in certain books.
(I'm paralysed with fear at the sight
of his ragged lips: they
threaten me
with absolute love;
they have shown me
how a symphony can be invaded
by cockroaches.) Let the two of us
drain this lake, he whispers,
let's hang ourselves together
on the hook of intransigence.
He kisses my nights
to confusion
that can only be fashioned
into barbed wire.
Then he falls asleep and snores
in my grammar
and I become
an orphan child.
Only when suddenly
he stumbles
very close to the horizon,
he turns yellow and shakes
and shouts that he's sick
of the heroism
that keeps me alive
and no more.

Love poem as it may come off

Dialectic comes between us and suddenly grows one more hump.

Clearly, there's no sense in asking you whether you can hear
the town's clocks howling for equilibrium. It's better I should
        kiss
your past week event by event, because the rosy cheeks of brave
        options wither
without a little warmth. I mean it, the blind man decked with
        baubles (who
I thought kept walking in my mouth pulling up from the roots
the same error again and again) doesn't even exist
and you're right, too much reading does eventually change
the sensitivity of the retina. I'm sorry but now and then
death or impotence or the voice of the neighbours swathe
my beliefs in barbed wire and it then takes entire seasons
to nurse them back to life, almost completely forgetting
the greatness of the daily bread that you honestly earn.

For our well-being's sake I promise to indulge my sense
of reality as I would a baby, to weigh it daily
and show it the cardinal points of disorder, I promise
to spoil it even though I have sometimes confessed
that I am struggling in a mass grave where
there's room for not even one more word.

Much later

Once I used to slap without pity
the mouth of the volcano.

Now I hardly dare breathe
under the story's
golden boots.

About all this,
someone will speak
much later
and someone else
will say that they're lying.

Straight to Olympus you'll go

Turn around to face the few remains
of the nimbus. History sweeps with clenched jaw
past your name. Are you scared
to pretend you don't care? Are you scared?
A pair of claws is growing, look,
growing with a smile in the mirror. Watch what you're saying:
a swarm of flies, the first ideals, deserters
and phantoms, all will declare
they've never seen you before.

This year in the month of March

The end lies further ahead, that's all. The prospects
have sometimes turned to face me too, speaking
their language and jumping from one thing to the other.
In the evening I watch the political map of the world
and can't make much sense of it, creatures of all sorts
do their own thing in the sarcastic ruins
of memory, I feel fine, naturally, what an uproar
on the anniversary of nothingness, oh yes, I order
the magnet to descend from around my forehead
and it does so, I order a fiction
to rot in the doorway, in the dark passage, as long as
from the height of this age that's so dear to me
thunders are heard and lightning flashes and rain holds off.

Ștefoi: translated from the Romanian by Oana Lungescu.

YUGOSLAVIA

GOJKO DJOGO

Gojko Djogo was born in 1940 in Vlahovići and studied comparative literature at Belgrade University. His poems are a tonic against power, a wise distillation of folklore set against post-war rule. He was the first Yugoslav writer to be imprisoned for poetry. In 1981 he received a two-year sentence for publishing *Woolly Times*. Protest readings were organized by the Writers' Union, securing his early release. *Woolly Times* remains banned.

The national hero

They cut off his left arm
and his right arm,
one, then the other leg,
finally his head
and they planted his neck in the soil
– to grow.

Children and scapegoats
hang on his stumps.

The wooden handle

Here,
Take it home and give it to your wife
So she may bear you sons
Without hiding the best man behind the door.

Tie it between your legs
So that your pants won't be empty
That you have something to lean on
When you stumble
Or stick it up on the ridge of the roof
To protect you from lightning.

You will have a poker for the yule log
And a pipe in your mouth.
You'll never find a better candlestick.
If its flame does not lick you
You'll take your Communion in the dark
And break your fast.

Take it, take it, you'll need it.
Whoever possesses the golden faucet
Will be the emperor's wine taster,
Whoever walks with a linden stick
Won't go to Constantinople on all fours.

If you fall to your knees, mount!
Bare-headed, in a bad mood
He boils stones
And saves the eggs for you.

He looks like you, too.
Could be your twin brother
A substitute in bed, at the church fair.
Just lend him your cap

And kiss his star-studded brow.

Here, take it,
Gouge out your eyes with it
And they will lead you home blind.

The black sheep

Here is the black sheep, master
Black are both her father and mother
Beneath her a black lamb
Sucking black milk.

And her blood is full of smoke
And her teeth are eye-teeth
And her eyes are cross-eyed
And she has horns
But no star on her forehead.

Whoever she kisses
Will catch the pox
In front of whosoever's house she dwells at dawn
His noon will grow dark.

Whether you lure her or not
She will not lick the salt from your palm
Nor manure your barren fields.

She prefers the wolf to the shepherd
She prefers the slaughterhouse to the sheepfold
And the blind leader
To the clairvoyant bell-wether.

– Hold out your hand to her,
You will have black on white.

Ovid in Tomis

Whoever lived
celebrated his birthday
– you who refused to live
waited for his end.

Your time has gone for ever,
because it was his time,
better not to have lived
than to have lived with him.

So lived mutes, toadies,
town criers and dupes, bootlickers, turncoats,
sycophants and lice,
so lived all those who were content
to have served his time
– only you refused.

One doesn't live a lifetime
waiting for another to vanish.
Who counts the days
counts his own.

> So many crosses turned into chips,
> torn boots and holy writs,
> crowns and sceptres rot in museums
> – one day his star will fall
> and children will push it with their fingers
> over a cushion in a showcase.

And what have you gained?
After us, no one will know
that Caesar wore
horseshoes on his feet.

Gold fever

Our roads are straight,
we've straightened all the curves,
the Stone Bridge slightly limps,
so we'll bury his left leg

and he'll get his golden badge.

Our corn cribs and barrels are full,
after gathering three harvests,
our grapes are not sweet enough,
so we've bought sugar on time,

he has earned his golden badge.

Our cattle are fat,
could survive the winter without eating,
pilgrims have brought foot-rot from Asia,
but we're vaccinated against the East,

and he received his golden badge.

The game fly to the gun-sight,
so we've salted a mountain goat's tail
for our esteemed guest to slaughter,
– now we'll have the finest antlers in the world

and he'll have his golden badge.

We're better off every day:
making tiny men from chewing gum,
they stretch and shrink between our teeth,
one woman received twins,

he received his golden badge.

Maquis

O maquis, the wolf yard,
give me insight into your laws,
teach me to eat
thorn and hawthorn,
to entertain guests,
beasts and vipers.

Instruct me from whom to flee,
in front of whom to bow,
not to mix with
anyone but pitch blackness.

Your pack is the last sanctuary.
I sharpen my wolf teeth,
and wait for the Stone Age
to return,
the infancy of the world
in our rotten garden.

Djogo: translated from the Serbo-Croatian by Michael March and Dušan Puvačić.

TOMAŽ ŠALAMUN

Tomaž Šalamun was born in 1941 'in a wheat field snapping his fingers'. He lives in Ljubljana and is the author of twenty books of poetry. *The Living Wound, the Living Juice* was published in 1988, and his selected poems were issued by the Ecco Press in the same year. Šalamun's poems invite a revaluation of all values.

Proverbs

1   Tomaž Šalamun made the Party blink, tamed it, dismantled it, and reconstituted it.

2   Tomaž Šalamun said, Russians Get out! and they did.

3   Tomaž Šalamun sleeps in the forest.

Translated from the Slovene by Tomaž Šalamun and Anselm Hollo.

Jonah

how does the sun set?
like snow
what colour is the sea?
large
Jonah are you salty?
I'm salty
Jonah are you a flag?
I'm a flag
the fireflies rest now

what are stones like?
green
how do little dogs play?
like flowers
Jonah are you a fish?
I'm a fish
Jonah are you a sea urchin?
I'm a sea urchin
listen to the flow

Jonah is the roe running through the woods
Jonah is the mountain breathing
Jonah is all the houses
have you ever heard such a rainbow?
what is the dew like?
are you asleep?

Translated from the Slovene by Tomaž Šalamun and Elliot Anderson.

Folk song

Every true poet is a monster.
He destroys people and their speech.
His singing elevates a technique that wipes out
the earth so we are not eaten by worms.
The drunk sells his coat.
The thief sells his mother.
Only the poet sells his soul to separate it
from the body that he loves.

Translated from the Slovene by Charles Simic.

Death's window

To stop the blood of flowers and rotate the order of things.
To die in the river, to die in the river.
To hear the heart of the rat. There's no difference
Between the moon's and my tribe's silver.

To clean the field and run as far as the earth's edge.
To carry in my breast the word: the crystal. At the door
The soap's evaporating, the conflagration lit up the day.
To turn around, to turn around once more.

And to strip the frock. The poppy had bitten through the sky.
To walk the desert roads and drink shadows.
To feel the oak tree in the mouth of a spring.

To stop the blood of flowers, to stop the blood of flowers.
The altars look at each other, eye to eye.
To lie down on a blue cabbage.

Translated from the Slovene by Charles Simic.

Words

You catch water with a pin,
the water turns to slush.
You point at the tree with your hand,
the tree burns.
You divide lines with a shadow.
You open the door for love and death.

Translated from the Slovene by Tomaž Šalamun and Anselm Hollo.

Eclipse II

I will take nails,
long nails
and hammer them into my body.
Very very gently,
very very slowly,
so it will last longer.
I will draw up a precise plan.
I will upholster myself every day
say two square inches for instance.

Then I will set fire to everything.
It will burn for a long time,
it will burn for seven days.
Only the nails will remain,
all welded together and rusty.
So I will remain.
So I will survive everything.

Translated from the Slovene by Veno Taufer and Michael Scammell.

NOVICA TADIĆ

Novica Tadić is a poet of distorted worlds. He was born in 1949 and lives in Belgrade. Tadić's poems create a mythology dominated by horror. Values are reversed; underprivilege resides beneath the surface of reality. 'The Nibbler' and 'The Dark Climber' are some of the bizarre characters that haunt his poems. *The Laughing-Stock*, his seventh collection of poems, was published in 1987; his selected poems appeared a year later.

The cats' strike

The cats' cough wakes him at night.
He turns in bed, gets up.
Puts on his dressing-gown because it's cold.
Puts on his slippers because he's barefoot.
Slowly approaches the window.
Drawing open the curtain, stares:
Below,
In the street,
As far as Republic Square
Thousands of phosphorescent flares
Thousands upon thousands of cats
Thousands upon thousands of raised tails.
Calmly
He closes the curtain.
And returns to his warm bed.
Yawning
he mutters:
                    – The cats' strike.

A small picture catalogue

1

In a dead town
dogs roam
among their own corpses

2

in a blind alley
a boy rolls
the halo of the Holy Mother

3

in a courtyard
a crucified
hen

4

in a brothel
smoke drifts
from a client's pipe
– a black stocking

5

in an entrance hall
shoes coats
hats gloves
a deserted house
never
        a human face

6

infinite grey
unknown forms above the water
salvation

At twilight

At twilight
  When I am bored
I imagine my murderer

That ant
Drags fire along
  Drags water along
    Drags black earth along

A conversation

One of the Cyclopes
met me in the street and
asked
      where was my
where was my
where was my
other eye little eye

I don't have it
I don't have it
I don't have it
It never
Opened

The icicle

The icicle is a crystal-woman
cold sweetheart
I know all about her because she is
my darling

In the old park we meet
secretly
under the trees

And her sorrel maids
squirrels
come   down

To eat something
as well

Dice

I rolled
Dice
On a table
Cut from black marble

No spots
No numbers
Nothing
There

ALEŠ DEBELJAK

Aleš Debeljak 'takes up the existential trend of Slovene poetry but sets it as an aspect of the contemporary self'. He was born in 1961 in Ljubljana and is presently studying social thought at Syracuse University, New York. His fourth collection of poems, *Fearful Minutes*, was published in 1990. Debeljak's poems rummage through the dictionary of silence, descend in a post-modern diving-bell.

Without anaesthetic

Things are empty. Containing nothing. As though they were the
    fruit
of some aborted plan. The landscape lies submerged in water
green from an unknown vegetation. Shadowed by the outlines
of the horizon. Filled with an emptiness everyone fears.

This morning just may smell of jasmine tea. That's not to
say it has some meaning. You may continue your
walks along the beach: that changes nothing. Everything within
your range of vision is just a bitter phantom. Recalling

images of events you know so well. You'll never
find the space for things. That last longer than your
fantasy, your hopes and secrets. You're surrounded by these
    things.
That's really not so bad. They're all that you can count on.
    They are.

Outline of history 6

Morning, when each of us has less sugar in the blood.
Morning, when day's whiteness smears across the windowpane.
Morning, when sleep achieves its peak, and it's not far now
to the river's mouth. Despair draws us out of sleep's ashes. My

morning is no less simple. Again I'm flesh and blood. The down
    blankets
shed. The last millisecond of waking has been arranged ahead of
    time. Like
everything that's taken place today. The arteries surge. And
one's field of vision flickers in anticipation. I'd rather not

resort to symbols. They're not what matters. There's time for me
to conceal the things that count. Warm from touching here, and
    there.
Shining colder than a star imprinted on one's cranium.
Not fading like footprints of a dead age, and this poem.

Forms of love 5

On that last trip you'd had no revelations.
The early morning when you returned – a flood of memories
of the Jewish quarter, and a kiss. The woman's shadow will
remain for sure. And Venice's deceptive play of

supernumerary echoes. And now you're lost. A dark flower
growing in your stomach's hollow. That vanishes in madness
as water does in water. There is no other life, that much is
clear now. And though the trip is done, the tension in your thighs

and brainpan won't diminish. You can't be seen. You're nobody.
With the features of an animal before it slips into darkness. An eye
        that
flashes toward the sky now and then. Outside, the sound of
        children
playing. Far off. Not here. Silence. And the light inside your room.

Forms of love 6

Listen, she began. A deathly silent labour, in which
I'll give birth to something greater than myself. Get ready for the
south-west wind that makes people sick, anticipate
a formless noise of passions, love, demanding poems,

sins. You'll understand: without me you'll never make the
      anthology
of blurs of light. If it weren't for meeting me, you would have met
no one else. A thought that may well take your breath away. But
      for all that
is it any less so? When describing you, my voice is warm, even

if I speak quite softly. Because you pulsate with my heart.
Because your veins conduct my smile. And the image that goes
with you overseas will be saturated with me. That which
      transcends me
is us, our moss, silver, vulnerability, endless journey.

Outline of history 7

The same nightmares, same addiction to alcohol, same
waiting for an eternal elsewhere that will take
shape in a solution made from man-of-wars. Like a poorly
pressed engraving, spraying the scorpion

venom that's etched in it nowhere. So that here and there
it mixes with the lymph of someone who can sense the
world's white sadness. Stretched taut in the still air. Enduring.
Like a dolphin on its circuit through the oceans. Submerged
    among

strained senses, bitterness, tears and flight are burning. And
everyone hides on the margins of night like frightened beasts.
    And
everyone presses his eyes shut, but it's no help. By the seventh
    day
the whole game crumbles into scenes from daily life.

Debeljak: translated from the Slovene by Michael Biggins.

BULGARIA

LYUBOMIR NIKOLOV

Lyubomir Nikolov was born in 1954 in the Vidin region of Bulgaria. He studied journalism at Sofia University and works at *Literaturen Front*, the weekly journal of the Writers' Union. In 1987 his second collection of poems, *Traveller*, caught many off-guard with its fresh, almost oriental brushwork – a Scythian cup in unpredictable hands.

Aladzha Monastery

for Kiril Borisov

And so we entered into the Moon . . .

The catacombs all round
are craters.
The sand is the colour
of crushed skulls.

Somewhere below us
smoking trees.
Somewhere below us
spreading foliage.

Below it perhaps
are angels.
Below it perhaps
are cockchafers.

Perhaps.
Anything is possible.

Valley of the roses

Yellow carts. Wet horses
and lavender – mist
over the field.
And nearer still to the sun the bees
have sunk their heads
into the jasmine.

Your face is fragrant among the roses.
A train passes.

And we might not have been here.

And your breasts
might have risen
among other fragrances.
And the sweating horses,
the bright carts
might have been visions
for another in the mist.

Beyond the field
a train whistles.

The rails start singing in the jasmine,
the bees are swarming over the sleepers.

Sometimes coincidence is all.

Morning

The universe has fallen fast asleep
like a young bee in last year's dark-brown honey.
But God's gracious hand
touches each bee-hive, one by one.

And bees are buzzing in the rosy darkness.
Above the wild thyme hangs a blue-haze sheen.
O moments before dawn, when life
seems bearable again.

Grandfather Nikola's oxen

Oxen like fishes.

Slowly we enter the earth.
They float above,
heavily, heavily.

Their days are the leaves under the nut-tree.
Their years are grapes in a barrel.

They pull everything:
the plough,
the war,
the state.

They will pull up a drowned idea.

Horseshoes get worn down.
Not oxen.

And I shout:
'Hey, Rizhko, Belcho,
we're barefoot, all three of us.
The stubble's pricking us.

Let's travel through the air!'

The valley

for Andrey Andreev

You're weighed down
by the light
flowing over the hills,
and the air –
like splashed lead –
pressed you
to the ground.

Everything weighs you down.

Clouds full of rain and seed.
The river, long and sinuous as a fish.
Stones with inscriptions
no longer legible.

Your nostrils drink in the valley air.
Horses and dragonflies in the meadows.

This cradle
suspended from
the sun and the moon
rocked your father
and his father –
whole regiments of fathers –

now it is empty.

And in the silence
I heard
words which your grandfather
heard from his grandfather,
and he from some
even earlier ploughman:

Boy, remember that the valleys
are grassy casting moulds
into which the Lord
poured our mountains.

A wandering of roots and branches.

It is time we came to our senses.

It is time
the river returned to its bed.

Inscriptions to the stone.

Ploughmen to their furrows
and the worm to the fruit
on the tree.

It is time
for the fruit
at last
to descend
into its root.

'All day'

All day I've shaken nuts down. No hands
left now to beat another branch.
And so I watch how, lighter than a feather,
a yellowed leaf is spinning in the air.
It spins, it waves about, it trembles
under the sun, drunken with happiness.
My withered leaf, how slowly you are falling,
how slowly you are falling,
how slowly falling.

Nikolov: translated from the Bulgarian by Ewald Osers.

VLADIMIR LEVCHEV

Vladimir Levchev was born in 1957 and lives in Sofia. He is the author of five collections of poetry. *Eighteen Poems*, published in 1989, displays a rare political maturity. Levchev works for a publishing house and edits *Voice*, a *samizdat* magazine for literary and political issues. He is a member of the Bulgarian Independent Literary Society.

Alone on the shore

1

I have not cried for years.

I am corroded inside by salt,
rotten from harsh tides.
I am a fish which carries
the sea within.

2

I watch the sunrise over the grey sea.
I watch the cold stars high above the spume.

I've walked along this shore for years . . .

3

My tongue is heavy.
My tongue's a breakwater.

Water and salt slowly destroy it.

In the end
the inexpressible swoops down.
Spume will be lament
and word
in the shell of night.

Theology of hopelessness

God is something very
small
and transient.

It trembles inside us.

Outside is death.

But if a man
sings out
when stood against the wall –
isn't he greater than death?

For isn't man
stood against the wall?

Let him sing!

The refugee

1

Every minute
has its countless cities
and skies
briefly illuminated clouds
windows lit by the sunset . . .
Every minute
has its secret corridors
leading to dark rooms.

Who lives there?
What would we have said to each other?
How would we have lived there?
I don't know.

Every minute
like a refugee
I walk past
endless doors
to eternal life . . .

2

We are guilty, my soul,
of knowing
about our loneliness,
about the end.
We are guilty.
And are expelled from Paradise.
The clock with its two swords
stops us from returning
through the minutes' path
to Eternity.

Stalin

(Saturn – Satan)

He said:
Believe in me! I am time!

And when they believed in him
he devoured his children.

Athens

Late at night you're in a strange house with wooden ceilings and cupboards, with a fragrance of age and olives. Under a flickering red lamp a woman – beautiful and soft – lies half-nude in damp sheets, regarding you. In the room sleepy people with yellow feverish eyes are talking. But she is waiting for you. Her eyebrows meet over her nose. She has three black nests under her armpits and between her thighs . . . While you're waiting to be alone with her, the woman changes her features. When she is tender, green-eyed, with a body like a sea breeze at sunset, you remember her, you love her . . . When she has black eyebrows she winks, she shows you her full breasts . . . And at times she laughs like a nervous youth . . . You listen: the Owl – seeing in the dark – feeds on the mice of madness.

Outside in the hot green night large snowflakes are driving. It is August. A clatter of necklaces of coloured bulbs and Christmas toys amidst high thoughts . . . The sea enters Athens, carrying ships from the harbour . . . Someone is calling for help. Outside, in the snow, you're woken by the heat of the body. The woman with the changeable face is already naked in the wind. Rapturous is the impending disaster! The woman regards you fixedly, in silence. She half opens her soft lips. You feel the pulse of the frightened white bird in the black nest. Her thighs embrace you and the sea engulfs you.

Do you understand why Socrates drank his poison fearlessly two and a half millennia ago? When the Owl broke his head with its beak – he was kissed.

Levchev: translated from the Bulgarian by Ewald Osers.

EKATERINA YOSIFOVA

Ekaterina Yosifova was born in 1941 in Kjustendil and studied Russian philology at Sofia University. She has worked as a teacher, dramatist and journalist and currently is an editor of *Struma*, a literary magazine in Kjustendil. She has published five collections of poems. *Names* appeared in 1988. Yosifova's poems make a sharp incision in love's shadow, where 'the soft dark and the hard dark fuse together'.

Or the other way round

Who should I complain about
or the other way round.
Aren't people born every moment,
able to breathe smoke instead of air.
They spell out their cold language of survival.
They rely on all kinds of machines
as on their relations.
The sun rises for them,
painted with signal paint.
Their brains are racing, their movement is perfect.
These are our horrible children,
the children of refugees,
and our nostalgias do not touch them.
Girls and women,
boys and men, freed prisoners –
in vain does our love pursue them.
We missed each other in the same streets
and we won't meet them again.

Golden anchors

With age some other things become inappropriate,
like poetry, at least up to a point,
the peacock's cry, the wings of love.

Not that I've lost a taste for pleasing others,
but loneliness, even so, is a condition
for seeing clearly.

And life is guilty, the enchanted place
where trivial hopes overshadow
great longings.

Everyone's mapping out his course,
though something else
makes us crowd together.

If only we knew its name.
But there's no one to ask,
the gods don't know it either.

An immense eye, a sightless
pupil. The soft dark
and the hard dark fuse together.

Only love's golden anchors
gleam nearby.
Beyond there's not a trace of a single soul.

Increasing verbosity

One way or another
man is The One who talks to himself.
Echo doesn't ring long.

Truly, words make me dizzy,
but after I'm silent for a while I am all right again.
And hints of a shared life make me uneasy.
What do you want to hear?

I know a few things already.
I know about children: giving birth doesn't mean self-
    perpetuation.
I know how important it is to submit to success.
And that the fact I'm here by accident doesn't relieve me
of duties.

If you're a man I'll confess to you that men are innocents.
But how they shine as wretched stars in the female sky.
The universe is for those who
don't look beyond their spell.
If you're a woman you've no need of consolation
elsewhere.

What kind of *au revoir*? I'd wish for you
that all life passes you by and that you smile,
just slightly twisted by the earth's attraction.
That this may be a brief encounter between us
across a distance:
a silence and a wind in the trees, where now
the light flits like a bird.

'If I had not dissipated myself'

If I had not dissipated myself so much
I might have grown old by now.
This age suits me well: one house comforts you,
one tree supports you,
everything supports me.

If I concentrate I'll remember what I have lost.
I haven't lost it, it just got lost.
I don't remain, my life remains.
So long as I don't forget what I considered important
at the beginning.

Others come and go, but that too is
through the strength of love.
Apart from that at every step something
is waiting or coming, and there's but one danger:
you being a child unhappy in a room full of toys.

Then it's like this: you're standing on one bank and look
across to the other.
And the running water makes your head swim.
What was important then?
If I concentrate I'll remember.

Only the water moves, the bed is dry,
hollowed some time by floods of love.
Must I traverse them all to know
where they lead to?
Grass grows, thorn grows, the cosmic beetle moves.

I could by now have been far away in the direction
which has ceased to be my own.
And this day, which now lazily flows between my eyelashes,

could have been short to the point of despair.
If I had not dissipated myself so much.

Yosifova: translated from the Bulgarian by Ewald Osers.

BOYKO LAMBOVSKI

Boyko Lambovski was born in 1960 and lives in Sofia. He was one of the founders of 'Friday – 13th', a club of poets opposed to socialist realism in the arts. *Messenger* won the award for the best début collection of poetry in 1986. He translates French and Russian poetry and lectures in literature. Lambovski's poems veer towards criticism, but instinctively return to joy.

'Marina'

Marina, our holidays are our punishment.
Our holidays are merciless exotic suns,
suddenly rising and suddenly setting,
and shame burns our faces.

Marina, our holidays are fragments
of the days when we were gods.
Love is a test to remind us
that we are wholly mortal.
And yet not wholly.

Which is why we must not pass each other by
as a miracle passes by
unbelieving eyes.
Let us once more, for a minute, be overwhelmed!
Let us for one minute be silent as a bell!

Marina, our holidays are our shame . . .
They make us great and we make them pitiful.
What's terrible is not that I am left alone.
The most terrible thing is that I love you
too little.

As the pencil dances over the paper

Thus a child pulls off
a doll's head
and from curiosity rips off
a tank's turret,
cuts an unread magazine
into strips
and builds
castles in the sand.

Thus an uncouth savage
angrily re-examines
the gnawed bones
after a finished meal.
Thus he looks askance
at his sleeping brothers
and with droppings of bats
he defiles the limestone.

Thus does a pensive Caesar
frown and scowl
before making an imperious
hypnotic gesture.
And cities are born
and tribes perish,
and someone curls his lips
with scepticism.

Thus a young man in love
walks down a lonely path
while emotion with terrible force
grows in his breast.

Thus grows the grass.
Thus grows the universe.
Thus life with measured tread
dances on death.

Fable of the Delphic Oracle

The day we heard
        that the ill-favoured slave Aesop
        was rattling on with his senseless parables
        before the people in the square
we simply walked away.

The day we learned
        that the impudent slave Aesop
        was accusing us of greed
we were astonished.

The day we killed
        the repulsive slave Aesop
no one came to the temple.

The clay man

Doctor,
what shall I do
with the clay man?

He doesn't want to learn.
The letters, he says,
make my eyes water.

His eyes are
like frightened drops.

They won't take him in the army.
With boredom the recruiting board
discovered a dove-grey
infection in his brain.

He won't do as a fool:
his smile
trembles
badly,
trembles to the right
trembles to the left.

Doctor, what
shall I do with the clay
man?

The doctor puts his hand to his forehead.
Earth after drought – that's his forehead.

The doctor doesn't believe
in God's know-how.

The strong man doesn't believe in the weak.

The fish doesn't believe
that the net will entrap it.

The sick man doesn't believe
in the healthy.

The tree doesn't believe
in the saw.

The living doesn't believe in the dead.

The clay man
doesn't believe in the doctor.

Lambovski: translated from the Bulgarian by Ewald Osers.

CZECHOSLOVAKIA

SYLVA FISCHEROVÁ

Sylva Fischerová was born in 1963 in Prague. She is currently studying Greek and Latin at Charles University. Fischerová is the most promising Czech poet since the Prague Spring. Her first collection of poems, *The Tremor of Racehorses*, appeared in 1986; *Large Mirrors* will be published in 1990. Her poems dance over ideology, though they are deeply conscious of present events. Under her spell myth regains its sweet lament.

Necessary

What was necessary
    we did.

The fields lay fallow
    and we ploughed them,
    sowed the grain
        and waited.

Our women lay fallow
    and we did what was necessary
    and waited.

When foreign riders came
    we did what was necessary
    fenced off the fields and houses,
    sharpened axes and knives.

But at night the riders
        jumped the fences
        on their high horses
        and played the flute
        under our bedroom windows.

We put up higher and higher fences
but the horses grew
                as fast as the fences
                and the flute played on.

Then our women left us
        and took the children with them.
        We did what was necessary
        burnt the remnants of their dresses,
                        the flowers behind the windows
and waited.

But no one has come.
                        The stoves are cold,
                        we go on waiting.

Maybe we've done less
                        than was necessary?
                        Or more?
And what if earlier,
before the riders came,
we had done less or more
and now we've done
                        enough,
but that's why
we can't wait to see,
since only the one
who does less
                        or more
waits and sees?

We don't know what to do
or whether to wait,
for by waiting
                        we're doing something.

Or aren't we?
    We don't know what is necessary.
        And the stoves are cold.

'In you there was a dark potency'

In you·there was
a dark potency
you were like ginger
            and fish,
            ice cubes
            a dessert called 'Delicious Death'
eager to do good
implacable in offence

Like a priestess of white magic
you damned redemption and suicide
            and books
   With your voice of old reeds in a young wind
   With your starry tobacco eyes
            and passion for the fateful
   In the end remained
            only sudden soothing
            touches of wind
            or
            'today a particularly ultramarine sky'
            and many long-past perfumes
                that always brought
                tears

Black tiger

Sometimes
there is only the black tiger
and the river with floating ashtrays.

Then
you throw away everything,
even yourself, gladly,
and you become
the black tiger on the floating
                              ashtrays.

You don't know why
nor what the black tiger and the river with the ashtrays
mean,

but it's a different ignorance
from
the constant fiddle with eternity,
from the black bottle of love,
god knows what's in it and
drink, man!

And the point is
that the tiger
comes only once.
Yes, and you look for him
always and everywhere,
        in black hair
        in black eyes
        in black vigils,

until suddenly
someone comes with candles
and then you are
again the black tiger,

only for a moment, so that at best
you can run away
and have eternity
stroke your chin
and say:
        You black tiger.

Am I my brother's keeper?

That was what he asked then
and there was a sudden heaviness upon earth like
        when a bird spits
           when a woman in bed turns her back
                        on a man.

We shall guard our brothers, you said
In that night of the Valkyries, fires and songs from Valhalla.
But even then you knew you were lying.
Even then you knew your love
was scarcely more than
           'not to lose self-esteem'.
Even then you knew that you were too many
for Him to condemn all.

    No one wanted that oath
      from you. And the eyes of the Valkyries
burn on in the darkness
          like gilded spittle
          like the Inquisition.

The merriest country in the world

He sat down and said:
> Play me the trumpet
>> as if it were a flute,
> play me the double-bass
>> as if it were a harp.

It was the best orchestra in the world.
> They played.

He said:
> Snap the strings
> and play a love song.

They snapped the strings
and the second violinist kissed
>> the violin.

He said:
> Play the Apocalypse.

It was the best orchestra in the world.
> They put down their instruments
> and stood with empty
>> hands.

He said:
> That is the first
> of the horsemen.
And before their eyes he burned the violas,
violins, drumskins,
melted the trumpets and cymbals.
> That was the second, he said.

And do you know
>   which is the third?
>   Under the rifle muzzles
>   to play their anthem.

>   And the fourth is
>   to play it yourselves,
>   without compulsion,
>   interlace it
>   with snatches of Mozart
>   and think that you've saved
>   something.

It was the dress rehearsal
in case of occupation.

After the occupation
they summoned the best orchestra in the world
and said:
>   Play waltzes, polkas, gallopades,
>   gallopades, polkas, waltzes.

>   For ages now
>   it's been the merriest country in the world.

The unfinished weight of the world

At times we catch the music of bones
    like the death of a beloved face
and lightly rub our eyelids,
      as if brushing away a night moth
          or a lifeless languor
          we can't be rid of.

And yet I wish I knew how
to walk among white beeches, aware
that it all depends on me,
      that moment
      under the lonely skies.
  That the Bible's message is:
      Do what you can, man,
      for what I have created is good.

  And then again
  the music comes,
  the singing bones of vanity,
  which divert
  my soul
      beyond the horizon,
      beyond that taut string
    for which anything
    is simply everything.
There I stand inert
empty-eyed
  inhuman
  like all who come to a place
      where you cannot weep.

And there, only there
I hear the crunching of fish spines
      deep in the mouth,
  the unfinished weight of the world.

Fischerová: translated from the Czech by Jarmila and Ian Milner.

IVO ŠMOLDAS

Ivo Šmoldas was born in 1955 in Prostějov, Moravia. He studied English and Czech language and literature at Charles University and works as a poetry editor at Czechoslovak Writers in Prague. His first book of poetry, *Winter Fur*, was published in 1988. Šmoldas's poetry is finely tuned to the harsher realities of modern urban existence. His sombre irony is tinged with pessimism, stoicism and playful wit.

Hour of the wolf

Under the lampshade
I stare at the books.
My winged ballpoint noses around.

And the books are locked
with thread and glue,
their spines stiffened during the autopsy.

All day I snapped
at my wife. Unleashed
my temper on the children.

And now the little angels
in their feathery clouds take revenge
by the innocent cruel measure of their breathing.

Winter children

In the dark behind the pasteboard door
the children sleep
under their feather hills
Morning is like stone

Heavy in their weightlessness
they go to the table
where the plates
gaze at the lamp's sun

The clock throws us out of the flat
I lead two shadows
to the nursery
and take off their coats

In the dark of evening
black as a stone quarry
they come home again

Under the pale sun where we are

Snapshot

In my memory's snapshot, now being taken,
our children are on their way to the village.

We wait for them at the hollow way
lined with blackthorn and stones.

Autumn in the vitals of things
shines in colour through the skins.

In times that have no present we stick to the future's
image of old memories.

The flash

Not much is left. Winter will soon be on us.
I rustle like a dry leaf.
And in the black earth behind your eyes
hate is sprouting.

I don't know what love is. It doesn't grow in me.
Yet anxiety grips me in its pincers
and plucks the features from my grey country
where you for ever live.

Šmoldas: translated from the Czech by Jarmila and Ian Milner.

EWALD MURRER

Ewald Murrer is a gardener by profession. He was born in 1964 in Prague and has published nine slim collections in *samizdat*. His poetry has distinct religious undertones, influenced by his brother who is a theologian. *Snakes under the Snow* and *Angel of the Grotesque* appeared in 1988.

'You are the one'

You are the one who will board the boat
you are the one for whom trees were felled
the wood smoothed
and shaped into a boat.

You are the one who will sail across the lake
you are the one hewn from fallen trees
who will sail on the boat
loaded with premonitions.

Where your journey ends
you'll gaze at a stone lighthouse,
mutely taking stock of things.
It knows, knows all,
but has no mouth,
doesn't hear your questions.

The water is black
full of fish shadows,
full of the bodies
of bulging thoughts,
of dumb queries.
Water full of water.

There the journey begins

Beyond the farmyard there's snow,
and from there the harnessed horses come.
That's where the journey begins.

The jingle bells laugh their laugh,
your hand holds an amulet of braided hair.

The horses don't face you,
their legs flash
but not a hair of the mane stirs.

The sleigh carries
your young body,
carries your ageless spirit.

Until now you didn't take that road
to the closed castles,
to the vigilant guards,
to the arena of battle.
Torn flags
haven't yet blocked your horizon.

And in your spirit you already see
how they carry you
like an old man
wrapped in blankets,
with the dignity of a defeated general.
And your fear they carry in their eyes,
the fear of an emperor
wandering lost through his chambers.

Twin skies

In the eyes twin skies.
One above the earth,
full of stars,
the map of pilgrims,
certainty of the way.

The other underground,
a black heavy sky,
full of diamonds,
the map of the lost,
last hope.

Gifts

He carries gifts,
he wishes to give beautiful gifts.
How to paint dreams on the sky,
how to slip words into the dark of the night,
how to weave words into a long rope.
Taut.
He carries clean sheets of paper,
as an offering to the hand beyond the horizon,
to the pen beyond the horizon,
that it may write before his eyes.

He carries gifts,
he carries his dreams.
A pack of good wolves,
the emerald gleam of a window on a distant black tower,
freezing plains,
quietly sliding sleighs,
a pale hand with rings,
a long face framed in flowing hair,
half closed eyes,
a hand spilling through the fingers
torn bits of paper.

He carries his dreams.

Murrer: translated from the Czech by Jarmila and Ian Milner.

JANA ŠTROBLOVÁ

Jana Štroblová was born in 1936 in Prague. She published four books of poetry before the Soviet and Warsaw Pact intervention of 1968. She was forced to leave her work as an editor of children's literature and was unable to publish for the next ten years. During the 1970s she did translation work under an assumed name. Her earlier poetry portrays a neo-romantic fascination with natural beauty, while her recent work reflects her experience of the crushing of the Prague Spring. *Witchery* was published in 1989.

To whom shall we leave our souls

They said to us:
>   the land is bad, no matter who owns it. You were rich
>   and you weren't happy.

>   You heard the battalions

>   and the brass bands, the dead still have their musters here
>   and among them living girls float like barques at sea,
>   at the concentration camp gates someone's selling hot dogs,
>   the public
>   has hung lights on the gate posts and waits
>   to see whether the dead are going to line up again,
>   and the dead are hungry, only compassion bends over them
>   like a young willow,
>   they still have to come here
>   because the public watches, indefinable as a face,
>   and how much time you spent on foot! Hunger divides
>   the murdered from the tourists,

>   you already heard the love

like a wave that seeks acceptance, like sounds,
it hummed like a receiver, beyond anyone's grasp,
you thought up boredom, larking and brawls, scaled the
    mountain by night

and you know every kind of touch,
no one's ever again going to die for a hair
or a single eyelash,
here there's no shooting and the world has too much time
to think about love
and expect disaster; formerly love made women grow into
    trees,

not now,
what else do you want? Illusions? And what kind?

You have listened to distance,
you also heard its drumming,
and someone broke his neck,
you hunted down the Moon and just for a while it amused
    you,
here there's no happiness, are you listening?

We're deaf!

The dregs of faith . . .

To whom shall be leave our deaf-mute souls?

Skin

I dreamt they ate
my neighbour
just
as for years they've eaten the flesh of the land
and now and then on the sly eaten one another
and buried the remains
It was bad enough   if only
a dream   The real thing
isn't much more tolerable
for after the killing and the bloody feasting
they would throw the entrails to the swine   You may say from
        thrift
No no   in an age when bread is wasted we don't break it   and
        whole
loaves are thrown straight to the devils
All they wanted was to vilify
In the end they tanned his skin and hung it on the gate
to drive away any pleasant dreams
of him returning
to me
And so from jealousy
the soulless deprived him of his soul

They wanted to take the soul
they took the skin

Soul and skin   Bloated with pride
they've no idea which of these is just a cloak
to be taken off
nor that there are unseen
regions
before which ordinary words are at a standstill
there on soundless paws memory
brushes through the foxtail under the Virginia creeper

and all the bounty of grove and deep forest
sometimes barks at cats screeching in the night
and then
in devotion turns back to us

And anyone who only now is shocked to grasp
that it wasn't a matter of human skin
should also know
why the noose of a mistake was tightened round his neck
Yes
they killed a dog like a man
Those who are always shouting: I'll kill you
like a dog

The drought

Besides heart failure, apoplexy, cataract,
eclipse of reason,
sprouting of tumours in the liver
and in the spirit, pollution
of the blood, thinning
of the bones and softening of vertebrae,
the country was suddenly afflicted with desiccation of the glands,
there was a lack
not only of milk but of saliva and tears, people had
cracked lips, the dried-up eyes
couldn't be opened wide nor even blink,
their fixed stare
was heavier than blindness.
And to be without tears is like being stuck
in the sun's furnace, not to be refreshed by shadow play,
not to pass through any shadows,
even one's own,
to give birth from another's womb – without pain,
not to recognize in tenderness its edge, in happiness its languor.
In dry weather drums were used to summon rain and crossbows
shot into the clouds. Now
the body snatchers drop artificial tears
into one's eyes.
Impossible to turn a blind eye: we see what happens
only too clearly. But it's no
optical illusion – or spectre; out of a dazzling white house
marked with a cross in blood, a first-aid centre,
another couple comes . . .
Yes, the woman refused
imitation tears for her eyes,
she's determined to find the real.
The times called for an incomprehensible event,
and shall have it. Eyes were turned up to the sky
in the hope
that the water would still be somewhat

pure,
and they let the rain
fall into them.

Circus

When the tamer,
　　mannequin of the ring,
arrogantly clicks his tongue
and the bear, god of the wilderness, statue
　　of his freedom, possessor
　　of the constellation,
humbly raises his front paws,
we know: it's the whip;
it has thrashed out every impulse to escape,
every growl of rage,
and the reward for good will,
the offered titbit,
is theatre, a showpiece to catch
the onlooker's eye.
We all know it – but we don't want
our money back,
we try to persuade ourselves we don't know
anything,
we clap with the simple children
when the bear pedals the bicycle,
blows up the balloon,
and when it comes to laughing, we laugh
even more,
and louder than the children,
because how can they know why
we laugh so much at
　　a fallen
star,
　　tamed
freedom,
　　a god
overthrown . . .
And we laugh most of all when with a final bow
the bear gently takes
the tamer's head
between its teeth.

The slaughterhouse

Certainly somewhere there's paradise
where the lamb sleeps curled up with the wolves and a man
buries his face in the lion's mane
but we are so far removed
that the butchers jauntily lash
the calf they're taking for execution
and skin the seals alive

Hold my hand while I tell you this
Pain hurts me I always shut my eyes
when in the cinema something bad
was happening

We shut our eyes
they open the slaughterhouse

Those who don't mind blood

And they trample a daisy a tree
kick a dog
and people
those they can kick
in the groin
The weak

The knife-edge of their denseness detonator of small-mindedness
and there is war
started by a bowstring tremor of the veins
by bad children playing the game of blood-flesh-bone

Don't shut your eyes

Hold my hand in this world

Štroblová: translated from the Czech by Jarmila and Ian Milner.

THE SOVIET UNION

ELENA SHVARTS

Elena Shvarts was born in 1948 in unholy Leningrad, where she has spent her life in its brick gardens. Her poetry, like the city's architecture, deploys mythologies for theatrical effect. During the pharaonic years her readings offered the city its own mythic cabaret. Now she has a wider audience, but her backdrop remains Russian Unorthodox. Her sado-masochistic heroines inhabit the same hyperborean space as the real patroness of Petersburg – the Blessed Xenia in a dead man's coat building a temple to Christ-Dionysos. *Points of the Compass* was published in 1989.

from *Cynthia*

I

Give me crimson ointment –
To calm the fever on my lips,
Warm my bed and give me
Hellebore in mulled wine.

Torrents of rain since morning–
With icy whips
Rome is lashed like a slave
Caught red-handed in theft.

The parrot shrieks in its cage –
The cursed thing won't stop talking!
Our countryside has frozen under a damp blanket,
Out there, however – far in the Pyrenees –

The legions are marching agaist the Germanii
Through ravines– they're like a little finger
That trembles long in the death agony
After the body itself has already grown cold.

No one of a more changeable nature than mine
Has ever been born in Rome –
Now, wherever my glance falls,
Everything irritates me –

The parrot keeps on squawking,
Pitiful present of a pitiful man,
Strangle it quickly, slave girl.
The little green body will afterwards swim in tears,
I will heap curses on you, but strangle it straight away now.

Gutters are howling – today nobody –
Neither thief nor lover will venture out of doors,
In vain the tavern opposite
Does not quench its turbid fires.

II

Father butts in again with admonitions;
– You shouldn't be living this way, he says, but that.
– Very well, daddy, I say to him,
I won't do it again, daddikins.

Meek and mild I look at his grey head,
His clawlike hands, his red red mouth.
I tell the slaves – this very moment
Hurl the halfwit into the fish pool.

He is dragged across the marble floor,
He tries to cling, there's nothing for him to cling to,
Blood flows down his face and with it tears:
– My own little daughter, he cries, forgive me, please!

No! the unfed moray eels shall tear you,
Lecherous bigot, mealy-mouthed prude.
Or I picture to myself – a lion
At the circus gobbling up his liver.

Alright, I say, alright – I'll change my ways,
Oh, you poor thing, my dear old daddy.
When a tiger had licked away even the scent of blood
I began to be just a little bit sorry for him.

In spirit I execute him variously – a thousand ways
And yet another thousand ways –
In the end, however, in actual fact,
The hammer raised – I never strike his temple.

III

How could you dare, slattern, how could you dare!
Too mild a punishment, exile to the country
Married off to an Iberian Celt
Who cleans his teeth with his own urine,
Or, as your soul's shade, to an Ethiop.
O you hussy! I was reciting Catullus,
Softly wandering through the house – and the lantern
Standing in the corner lengthened my shadow –
She came stamping in out of the kitchen
Heaving some mackerel on a gilded salver
And stepped directly onto my very – shadow –
Onto my head, and then onto my forearm!
And my shadow is more bruisable and tender–
Well she knows it! – than her padded hide is.
If they were to fry you in a skillet,
In the same one as the noble mackerel,
Even that would be less painful to you
Than it was to me – when your foot trampled
Into the floor – the shadow of my ringlets.

VI

Claudia, you won't believe this – a gladiator has fallen in love
     with me.
In the circus three seasons he has remained undefeated,
I am forty already, and he is still youthful and handsome –
He is chaste, honest, dark-skinned, enormous and sad.
A Hannibal's elephant bears fewer scars than he does.
At the circus, they say, he constantly watches for me
But never discovers me there – for I do not frequent it.
No sooner does dusk fall – at twilight he knocks on my door,
Sits out the evening propped on his sharp-glinting sword.
His breathing is heavy and strained through his mouth and his
     glances
Are passionate and piteous alike . . .
My lover laughs himself to tears about him.
Not, of course, to his face – for he, as you know, is a coward.
All the vices are united in him.
Glimpsing the gladiator he leaps straight out of the window.
'Passion – says the gladiator – is hindering me in combat,
If this should continue, I will not return to Gaul,
As it is my triumphs now lack their previous panache,
In no time some nimble upstart will slit my throat.'
What can he see in me? I cast cold glances upon him,
The deer-like gleam of his eyes, the swarthy and powerful arms.
What can I do, Claudia, Cupid is wayward –
Unfortunate that I am I love the bald monster
Who like a pitiful slave huddles behind the door
In order to cry out afterwards – chase that killer away!
Meanspirited, I would be sorry to throw him out,
When will another such hero love me again,
And how soon they turn into old fogeys.
The sated wolf still needs a sheep for the winter.
I prolong his anguish, but if – by his love exhausted
He should fall in the ring – how should I then live,
     Claudia, tell me?

VII

How I envy you, Bacchantes!
Lightly you cavort across the uplands,
The white of your eyes fragments the gleam of moonlight,
Like Mongol mares you canter.
Once I happened to be standing near you,
A friend had brought me, we were only watching –
Suddenly she surrendered, threw herself
Into a drunken dance and broke away
Hard in pursuit of you, forgetting me.
I looked on – your mouths were all contorted
And your faces twisted sideways
Like the masks of mediocre actors.
You tore apart a living bull
And falling on it, you devoured the flesh
And doused your bodies in its burning blood,
Swilling away all reason as a slave girl
In one gush might empty an amphora.
And from nearby I watched you.
Then I came home – and saw – my arms were scratched,
Bleeding all over, to the very elbows . . .
Such is your lot, unhappy Cynthia –
Upon yourself you may unleash your passions,
Upon yourself alone, and not the tiniest
Trace of passion will you allow yourself to show.
You will not pursue a bull, stark naked . . .

Animal-flower

Presentiment of life abides till death.
A chilling fire burns along the bones –
When a bright shower passes over
On St Peter's Day at break of summer.
Scarlet blooms are just about to flower
On collarbones, on ribs, upon the head.
The cluster will be tagged *Elena arborea* –
Its habitat is freezing Hyperborea
In gardens made of brick, in grass of stone.
Eyes sprout dark carnations. I'm at once
A bush of roses and forget-me-nots
As if a savage gardener'd grafted on me
A virulent florescing leprosy.
I will be violet and red,
Crimson, yellow, black and gold,
Inside a dangerous humming cloud
Of bees and wasps I'll be a sacred well.
And when my flowers fade, O Lord, O Lord,
What a bitten lump there'll be left over,
Grown cold and with its skin split wide,
A faded, half-dead Animal-Flower.

Shvarts: translated from the Russian by Michael Molnar.

ARKADII DRAGOMOSHCHENKO

Arkadii Dragomoshchenko, a Ukrainian, born in 1946 in Potsdam, was brought up in Vinnitsa. Although his adult life has been spent in Leningrad, he remains a stranger to its local myths. Dragomoshchenko's work is alien to Russian sentiment and its tradition of the 'poetical'. Instead, he weaves saying and seeing into his own idiosyncratic lyricism. His language is a retina that interprets bits of information. A drop of water, a swift's flight, tangles of roots – in his poetry natural phenomena mutate from objects into agents of perception. *Descriptions* appeared in 1990.

Lesson

There are days when the sky is open.
From daybreak a foggy disc touches the ground.
But in the heights, in feathers tinted gold,
With difficulty you can make out a star's
                              distant, incomplete appearance
Defined in unlit empty space
Still nothing but a point
Not yet sunk into the page of night.

Though perhaps that is the eye's offence.

But the sun is lower and it's harder for the gaze
To follow the muted sinking of the earth
Into the most sweet, confused and convoluted hour
So gently rotting through the coverlet of the day
That we are ready to compare it now
To some strange voiceless speech.

Be like a spectre. Hold your breath.
The south is a singing stone laid at the foot of the bed

And evening twilight's icy hand scorches the brow
Bringing an end to worries,
Closing the circle of work, beginnings, love

But suddenly obliquely severed rays
Flare out again. So high up! – you say.
They drop down at our feet where there is snow and – nothing
Where they dissolve again in emerald smoke
For the last time.
                    The raven locks itself
With an iron wing.
                        Then the house is like a frame
                                        charred by fire
In which we listen to voices,
Habitual liars at the porch of the night.

March elegy

. . .the rose . . . the snows
From the poetical

Collapsed and faded the crazy sheepfold of frost,
The solar cowl of the rose is pale as damp plaster,

Brother wolf with his ravenous belly is foraging through thickets
Along the ravines and among the sparse coppices,

Relentlessly baring his teeth at himself in the darkness,
Ears flush to his scalp, ruffling his scraggy hide and grieving,

He forages
In the black gullies, squinting an eye at the moon
Staring straight at a plaster doll amid the gold . . .
Nobody.

If only a filthy Tatar!
Oh, how faint and mournful the whining of stubble on the fells,
If only some elder would happen to cross his track –
He wouldn't insult him with help, just rip out his throat.
Nothing.

He sheds his fur in hanks, chokes on husks of froth,
Anguishes, a yellow fang in cascades of magical fumes,

It's not the moon that spatters his maw with frosty water,
It's not the plague star like a little sister that plucks at his heart,

Tearing his paws to the bone on the diamond snow-crust
Night and day
Day and night bent into a single bow,
A younger brother recalling Prince Ivan comes hurtling
Straight into the eye of the sun –

See what he's thought up, the skinflint!

from *Reversiya*

Emergence of a bird from the thought of gravity
Gravitation towards a pole – seizure
                                                    and falling
The hand's form
gravity

division of the bird into a faded shape
                                                    in the retina
cluster of moisture
breath of air on the face
spring showers

this long apprenticeship – belongings –
        to divide something into the consonance of hostility
into air   not culminating in any block
the persistence of thought around the barrier of memory
its accumulation
the route back

this long apprenticeship

When, why and to what end – No word.
But again, like a thousand times before,
Into our face the staircase splashes steps.
A delightful precipice.
                            And leads us back
towards the slope's beginning.
Drunkenness. The river. And a rose.
Under hesitant skin a clinkered sea . . .

And the snowbound year bursts in the windowpane by force
And such exquisite malice, an angel at the foot of the bed.

Sometimes it appears blue,
sometimes wet and green – that street lamp,
But you wake up: the west wind shifts
                              a sheer wall of snow
And your headache is like a little girl in a dress
                              faded from the wash.
She goes out, sinking up to the ankles in May sand.

A straw hat, tufts of coloured wool,
My hand scrawled over with black marker ink,
Rain jumbled up with snow –

On New Year's Eve I'll get myself
                              the dull rat's garb

and the word 'love'.

The flood of evening   a scourge
    childish shrieks in the delta

From a distance we observe
Nests of faceted deposits.

The far-off trees
Are singled out by the shape of their foliage
                                        the degree of its death

By the length   the green of the root
By the weave of veins
By the height
and by their links with ancient   too transparent
                                             languages

Nothing   in any way to single out
The nearer trees   more indistinct

Among them the acerbic decay of sound
Naïve the impression of a voice

Fire of bushes
Tree trunks' light wounds
Feathery clouds

Dragomoshchenko: translated from the Russian by Michael Molnar.

ALEKSEI PARSHCHIKOV

Aleksei Parshchikov was born in 1954 on the Pacific coast near Vladivostok, grew up in the Ukraine, the South and the Crimea and now lives in Moscow. *Figures of Intuition* appeared in 1989. Parshchikov's writing delights in the birth and growth of images, not in metaphors as such but in moments of metamorphosis. The switches of perspective are what matter, or the point in time which is out of time when desire animates mechanical toys and the future is impending fact.

August on the Dnepr

Sleep till August – it all comes clear through dreams
and the twilight there is timid because of the stars'
idiosyncrasies, pious faces of cold apples
gape at the little pendulums of the plums.

Bazaars break out in a chicken pox of berries
and you can leap through hoops of price tags
trading ripe insults among the trestle stalls –
as if you were acting – between the acts!

Stuck to windows, dried-out transparent pods,
Thermometers bare scales like vertebrae,
above the wharves in a salt sweat, heat
has touched its limit neck-deep in mercury.

Sleep till August! the moon's ellipse is crumbling
and in your footprints the sandstone shines,
fireworks stab upwards and hook back,
collapsed like flippers reaching for the sky.

Curled shavings of whinnying disturb your dreams
from fields of stubble shorn like conscripts,
out among the halberd reeds
the moon is moored to hawsers.

Mudflats

We trudge knee-deep through medicinal mud and never look
    back,
and the ooze sucks us down and its dead clutch is alive.

Draw a blank here, a joke, a ridiculous sackrace
littering funnels of slime behind us like smokestacks.

As ever, my angel, I love the rustling at dusk,
as ever I will offer you heather and hides,

but this is all just a whim dreamt up by the mudflats,
golden in the morning, wooden as a pipe at night.

Frail stalks and the dragonflies seethe with a velvet charge,
no route through the earth or sky, just a tangle of tracks.

Among these sickly waters that heave like a stretcher
there's no bridge or hill or star or intersection.

Just a rock like a thunderhead and both of them similar
to any point in a universe that's achingly familiar.

Just the wrench of a vista heavy as a punctured ball,
just a hole in the ground or simply the lack of a hole.

Transfer

Seized in time's light like an actor, back to the glare,
screwing my eyes against darkness, I peer out into charactered
    dark;
wherever I roam the figure of my intuition returns to the
    clairvoyant Djuna,

splitting me into a hundred fragments and sinking into the
    Kremlin;
no sooner come to, I notice I am standing amid those who look
    out
from the edge of the foundation; seven spheres make up the
    heavens.

Minarets of shadow rise over the audience's heads as if out of a
    bay
Cairo in twilight had entered the sector of vision
or the praesidium threaded from beneath on a low-power
    projector . . .

Applause and speeches, the session in progress transforms into a
    banquet.
The First person is here and the Sixth and between them a world-
famous mine is seated, its exhausted interior glaring.

The Fifth man protrudes his lip and synchronically wags his
    finger;
permanganic acid dissolves like a dancer dispersing
gaseous material across the auditorium: the Third slits his eyes.

I discerned a certain limit to their gradual movements,
was it trash or facetted crystal – a sharp little cube, it seemed
they had caught it right on the neck – just try and grab it!

This was a temporary failure of coordination like archival
    footage,
the auditorium cupola blinked like a bull knowing it's been killed.
I discovered the law of coincidence between matter and fate.

I loved the shore with its seaweed, neolithic beneath the moons,
and also when a full glass of cabernet is poured, radiant with a
    poppy rim . . .
No, I'm here, sinking deeper and deeper into the pyramids'
    bureaucratic gloom,

split into a hun fragments I shift as a swarm; the feast or
    whatever
it was transformed into a procession – all surge towards a tunnel,
jammed together like great corn-cobs they disappear into the
    shaft.

What did they carry, what did they conceal, what was their aim?
Spruce blue-hazed fir-coat, answer me that one point-blank!
They carried years of death and the bed of great horror.

Yes, they carried a leader, he could be split into pinches,
he could be split into pinches, pinches, pinches,
he could be transmitted along a chain, chain, chain,

he could be a grain in the cosmos and a part of your beauty,
whether you be land or maiden, no matter in the wilding word!
Splintering he could define himself down to the very void.

Like a trowel, space bent at the edges and – ouf! – in long-drawn-
    out
stages, benignly they lowered a cask with a mummy from their
    stately shoulders,
it lay, wedged awry. Here I sensed a subcutaneous

prod and – came to in Georgia. Dances. Another language.
Light a cigarette? You have dignity, I have freedom.
And the night switched on and off in the tiny horns of snails.

A jaguar lies on your shoulders, your cheekbones are gilded.
Everything's in order. No big deal? Look, through the gateway
like a lemon lens blazing in silk, driving up behind us comes a
      Lada.

New Year verses

Me, the Snow Princess and a rooster on a chain
                                        – meet the gang –
tour our folk, at a slight fee, round the sectioned
                                        face of a clock,
a boat segment sails off and abandons the circle.
                                        At New Year
clocks quit their housing and spin off like
                                        polka dots over the sky.
The glued beard gnaws my cheeks, you're tired,
                                        the hobbling rooster's done in,
we're a dog-eared card pack that'll cut
                                        at the king of spades,
doors open for us, kids are nudged in the back
                                        – guess who's come!

Lush wealth of champagne on the tables
                                        rustles like shimmering poplars.
Who's come, who's stepped onto the frozen globe,
                                        creating nothing, changing no names?
We swap gifts for three slices of toast.
The sack on the floor's like a sagging bust,
                                        like the rooster, like you, like me,
the sack shifts and tries to adopt
                                        the questioner's expression.
Kids hang around, their muscles tense,
                                        ears looped in their specs.
Toys tumble out of the sack.

Parshchikov: translated from the Russian by Michael Molnar.

VIKTOR KRIVULIN

Viktor Krivulin was born in 1944, when the siege of Leningrad was finally lifted. His poetry recycles fragments of epic history and literary myth as components of everyday life. Its true element is urban folklore, transforming banality into anecdote. Krivulin's map-poems are plans of his generation's cultural space-time; they are forays into a no-man's-land between conventional frontiers.

from *Poems on maps*

maps and calendars and maps.
time and space. time
of diaspora and dissolution
in the short dictionary of rhyme
in the blockades of besieged speech

let's leave a few names behind
the broken line of a frontier.
uncontoured, unconcerned by features
light streams from the plan, from the page
turning over us

some few of all the voices
I can hear: freed from the chorus
a nebulous stalk, it's a splinter
from woods exploded by the spring

some few of them over my head:
eyewash, a scumble of cloud.
on the historical tracks
some sort of half-way station

looming. a manuscript vault –
or rather, no dome but a hillock.
within it a chasm, but in our talk
the bluetit cannot even find the space

to weave a nest. how can one live one's life
more meagrely? – and speechless cross
to an artificial gallery
made of fretworked bone and sky

lemony-bitter strip of sunset.
what's limonov publishing at present
in the west where life is somewhat bitter
for the poet? at present what's he writing
to his friends – touching the tenderest or
most painfully sensitive chords?

above the rhetorical questions
above the allegory of Fortune
stretches out a longitudinal
sunset – in the palish afterglow
a triangular pediment shines yellow
with the Hermes of the pushkin house

with its alexandrian grimace.
but the Customs of a cultural phantom
(whatever we may talk about and
wherever, be it in New York or Rome)
are intolerable: on the backcloth
of the sunset, in the limelight, alas

poor limonov! bitter is the wind –
inside the drumhead of the pantheon
the library is established

news gets round. I see from the window:
a grey-haired poet, once a bloomsbury youth,
is crossing the street. above him
moves the diurnal moon –
sympathetic influence of the almost
hallucinated disc . . . saint Hieronymus
fondling a lion . . . but in all conscience this
never hung on any wall!
and news gets round as in sleep
bypassing brain and penetrating body
and skin responds at random
growing alternately tense and slackening
at the internal and external noise
extinguished in the sound of plainsong

Flight to Egypt

almost the moment almost
the place, the dead centre of crossed
wires in a gunsight – almost the place
but hard to wrest the spirit.
pursuit. and for some reason or other
glancing back to find
in april quattrocento air
and breath and rest on the road
to egypt. flight. the edge of the picture
shadowy and impenetrable

wellspring, an angel, an ass
a family fleeing beyond the frame –
all this to one side, but straight on
at the centre – sheer caprice
of targeted antique ruins
collapsing bole of a column
and in symmetrical sculptures
purple vine tendrils snake
braiding a hot thigh.
pursuit. the attendant

guardian in a hurry
to be at home stares at the last
visitors. through the summer
windows heat seeps inside
from the late afternoon – in the gallery
in front of a shadowy picture
Three remain. we at the start
of an unapparent path
almost the moment almost
a radiant Map behind our shoulders

Krivulin: translated from the Russian by Michael Molnar.

THE BALTIC REPUBLICS

<u>ESTONIA</u>

DORIS KAREVA

Doris Kareva was born in 1958 and lives in Tallinn. Her poems are delicate petals, the green living ash of eternal grace. Her six books of poetry include *Secret Consciousness* and a volume of selected poems, *Days of Grace*, to be published in 1991. Kareva's poetry is spare, often despairing, and displays an uncompromising ethical stance. 'A poem is like a dream – at once a memory and a fantasy; a genuineness that opens up not along the lines of life but the lines of fate; no, not the lot that befalls us, but an eternally present part of our world.'

'Your light shirt remained glimmering in memory'

Your light shirt remained glimmering in memory
as a sign of life,
as a mark amidst darkness
and chaos.

The day, when the sun escaped
its exile.

Leaves tremble,
a shadow moves on the road,
I am still alive.

'Clarity and secrecy'

Clarity and secrecy
meet in a darkening room.

Petal by petal,
love gives itself away.

'The night left a scent'

The night left a scent, living and dark.
The patter of rain tuned the high roof.
We spoke of the dead
and the miracle yet to be born.

Your eyes, they were close,
they breathed inside me,
illuminated the bottom of my soul,
my resurrection.

Dawn glowed at the rim of the sky.
And through the land of god
I wandered beside you,
too fulfilled to give thanks.

'To make one life visible'

To make one life visible,
and give it to many
to keep
is impossible.

There remains a distance,
there remains a tinge of estrangement.

Only deep wisdom,
spacious love,
draws closer and unites
our differences.

This spirit of
light and freedom
which appears at once
in two bodies

and recognizes itself
in both.

'Her quiet words let loose'

Her quiet words let loose a mass
of hysteria.

No, not enlightenment. A miracle
they wanted,
and at once.

She stood – lucid, calm and alone –
two heavens unexplained
and bare hands.

The wind floated her hair
and she laughed.

'There shall come no other
and better world'

There shall come no other and better world
for us. Just as no deed done
will change.

The wind and sky today are not the same
as yesterday.
No, no one to count on outside
our fragile borders.

Only light.

Kareva: translated from the Estonian by T. H. Ilves.

LITHUANIA

SIGITAS GEDA

Sigitas Geda calls his poems 'forgotten chronicles'. Born in 1943 in a small village in south-eastern Lithuania, Geda appears as an ancient shaman whose 'earthliness' shapes a wild, personal philosophy into a nation-state. *Green Beads of Amber*, published in 1988, is his eighth book of poetry. His archaic voice reverberates inside the Sajudis, the movement of national revival. 'Drink. Pray. Pray. Drink.'

The collective request of the dead country children from Pateru village

couldn't someone – turn into
small sparrows from our childhood –
and bring us – sour pears –
from Petrukas' old pear tree –
near the lake? –

the skulls in these graves – are so
big – but we were –
so small –

Spring in father's orchard
– an epileptic fit in childhood

an angel
reads
my
opened
book
each page
    each bluish
    syllable
who turns
its pages
in this
wind
    between father's
    white
    apple trees
so what if
I am three
years old
    I am already
    dead

Spring in Buivydiskes

and again
that same
wood lark
comes out
of the earth
the northern
spirit
cowering
in a green
egg –

a wood lark
that
was listened to
ten thousand
years
ago

entirely
not in this
world

the hymn
is the same –
forces
control
the universe

An epitaph by the blue waters

here
lie
christened
Lithuanians
having lost
the first
battle
near Vorksla

and
after that
they
lost
another
thousand
times

with
God

From a forgotten chronicle

the Russians
lived
at that time
in cellars
they
were
brown
they
could
only
eat
thrush
and sparrow's
balls

they no way
wanted
to climb out
afraid
of the Viking's
wolves
and the Balt's
thunder
from Kijava

'A wild lake'

A wild lake,
Original water.
Brown reeds
Smelling of our forefather's bodies.

Green grassy fish on the bottom,
Duck nests in the warm water
And four eggs.

A crab hides,
Covering itself with a shield.
Winter or summer –
No footsteps.

Oh green fish
On the green lake floor,
Dream me up
As fast as you can!

Geda: translated from the Lithuanian by Laima Sruoginyte.

LATVIA

JURIS KUNNOSS

Juris Kunnoss was born in 1948 and lives in Riga, working as a curator at the Open-air Ethnographic Museum. 'Everything is of use, everything that has not been seen, but has been read, thought, browsed and felt.' Along the dunes of Old Riga history throws *Five Seven*, his second collection of poems, published in 1987.

'They will have eyes to see'

they will have eyes to see and they will not see
neither ridges of mist nor fruitstone nor root
neither darkness of raven nor bleaching bones
will they see

they will have ears to hear and they will not hear
neither grass sprouting during the endless nights
nor the prophetic song of the honey-tongued nightingale
will they hear

they will have tongues to speak and they will not utter
a single word to river tree mist or stone
not a brass farthing in the name of hell
will they utter

but the wound of this field will not close
sown with dragon's teeth

A ploughman drowsing

round morning softer
and softer the wind flaps its wings

with such craftsmanship the carver furrows
a face in wood

the artisan is the salt of the earth
and the blacksmith tempers the spirit

he hammers the word like a mace
and yet like a cluster of birch buds

the carpenter bethrothed to his homeland
comes to hack out dwellings

the sun is transformed into rye
that sifts into silos

softer and softer
till everything falls silent

mopping his brow the stonemason
sculpts crosses

Nothing but summer

As in a fiesta
we flee across a green meadow
from the savage snorting bull clouds.
– – – we collapse
into the scent of grass, the bulls
trample us lightly.
We are saved, it's a miracle!
We visited Spain,
now there are other clouds waiting
and other lands.

'One more life'

one more life

black may night black night of Maya

a halo violet like a plum around the moon
star bubbles tumble from the grandest anvil
and leave a rustle and glitter in the wild rose bush

billion-year pulsars
                        shrunk to a clenched fist
                                                breathe

sifted through a sieve scattered through the mesh of a net
we are here upon this earth in time and space
but in a parallel universe live celts and prussians
and if their grass is without odour and their birds are dumb
rays of their sun cold as the icicle fish
do not grieve
pulsars breathe blood the dough ferments
sags and rises and flies off oh
                        the eternally shimmering salver

the coverlet woven by Maya a carpet or veil
have no fear of the forest and its dark sultry murmur
a bower surrounds the moon
                        one more life
lighting creation with darkness

'Sign with a streak of rain'

Sign with a streak of rain, sign with a gust
of wind when your fingers are crooked, when
your slight words can't restore light to a bird.

For a long time yet you will delay your decisive
steps, heap coals of fire on your head, become
birch bark, scatter pebbles in your trail.

All the same you've roads, ditches, bogs, ruts,
detours to traverse until your mouth drains the swamp
water, black fibber: then you'll become a whistle.

A bird will fly by and breathe into you. Yes, you've picked
your work: the stars will disappear, not disappear, turn
to grains in your chest, you will understand earth.

Kunnoss: translated from the Latvian by Michael Molnar.

SOURCES AND ACKNOWLEDGEMENTS

The publishers gratefully acknowledge permission to reprint copyright material in this book.

IOANA CRĂCIUNESCU: to Ioana Crăciunescu and Fleur Adcock (translator) for 'Shipwreck', 'Abundance in suffering', 'City without a biography', 'Chronical III', 'Her little red ear' and 'A thousand and one nights'.

ALEŠ DEBELJAK: to Aleš Debeljak and Michael Biggins (translator) for 'Without anaesthetic', 'Outline of history 6', 'Forms of love 5', 'Forms of love 6' and 'Outline of history 7'.

GOJKO DJOGO to Gojko Djogo and Michael March and Dušan Puvačić (translators) for 'The national hero', 'The wooden handle', 'The black sheep', 'Ovid in Tomis', 'Gold fever.' and 'Maquis'.

ARKADII DRAGOMOSHCHENKO: to Arkadii Dragomoshchenko and Michael Molnar (translator) for 'Lesson', 'March elegy'; 'Emergence of a bird', 'When, why and to what end', 'Sometimes it appears blue', 'A straw hat' and 'The flood of evening' – from Reversiya.

KURT DRAWERT: to Aufbau Verlag and Agnes Stein (translator) for 'Mirror symmetry'; Aufbau Verlag and Margitt Lehbert (translator) for 'Clearing up', 'Simple sentence', 'For Frank O'Hara' and 'Defence'.

SYLVA FISCHEROVÁ: to Sylva Fischerová; Edinburgh Review and Jarmila and Ian Milner (translators) for 'Necessary' from Edinburgh Review, issue 78/9; Field and Jarmila and Ian Milner for 'Black tiger'; Jarmila and Ian Milner for 'In you there was', 'Am I my brother's keeper?', 'The merriest country in the world' and 'The unfinished weight of the world' from *The Tremor of Racehorses* (Bloodaxe Books).

SIGITAS GEDA: to Sigitas Geda and Laima Sruoginyte (translator) for 'The collective request of the dead country children from Pateru village', 'Spring in father's orchard', 'Spring in Buivy-diskes', 'An epitaph by the blue waters', 'From a forgotten chronicle' and 'A wild lake'.

WOLFGANG HILBIG: to S. Fischer Verlag GmbH and Agnes Stein (translator) for 'You have built me a house', 'Awareness' and 'Absence' from *Abwesenheit*, © S. Fischer Verlag GmbH, Frankfurt-am-Main, 1979; 'Entrance' and 'The names' from *Die Versprengung*, © 1986 S. Fischer Verlag GmbH.

TOMASZ JASTRUN: to Tomasz Jastrun; Michael March and Jaroslaw Anders (translators) for 'The seed', 'The Polish knot', 'Nothing' and 'Fruit'; *Northwest Review* and Daniel Bourne (translator) for 'Scrap' from *Northwest Review*, Vol. 25, No. 2, 1987; *Greenfield Review* and Daniel Bourne for 'Hat'.

DORIS KAREVA: to Doris Kareva and T. H. Ilves (translator) for 'Your light shirt', 'Clarity and secrecy', 'The night left a scent', 'To make one life visible', 'Her quiet words let loose', and 'There shall come no other and better world'.

VIKTOR KRIVULIN: to Viktor Krivulin; *Bomb* and Michael Molnar (translator) for 'Lemony-bitter strip of sunset' from *Bomb* magazine; *Michigan Quarterly Review* and Michael Molnar for 'Some few of all the voices'; Anvil Press Poetry and Michael Molnar for 'Flight to Egypt' from *Poetry World I* (1986); Michael Molnar for 'Maps and calendars and maps' and 'News gets round' from *Poems on Maps*.

RYSZARD KRYNICKI: to Ryszard Krynicki and Michael March and

Jarosław Anders (translators) for 'How does it rise', 'It, sleepless', 'The beginning crossed out' '⁀ourney through death I', 'Journey through death III' and 'Ho˴ ˷ky it is'.

JURIS KUNNOSS: to Juris Kunnoss and Michael Molnar (translator) for 'They will have eyes to see', 'A ploughman drowsing', 'Nothing but summer', 'One more life' and 'Sign with a streak of rain'.

BOYKO LAMBOVSKI: to Boyko Lambovski and Ewald Osers (translator) for 'Marina', 'As the pencil dances over the paper', 'Fable of the Delphic Oracle' and 'The clay man'.

VLADIMIR LEVCHEV: to Vladimir Levchev and Ewald Osers (translator) for 'Alone on the shore', 'Theology of hopelessness', 'The refugee', 'Stalin' and 'Athens'.

PETER LEVY: to Peter Levy for four lines from The Psalms, translated by Peter Levy (Penguin Classics, 1976), copyright © Peter Levy, 1976.

BRONISŁAW MAJ: to Bronisław Maj and Adam Czerniawski (translator) for 'The silence in a house', 'In the forest at night', 'Seen fleetingly', 'Evening at Kraków Central Station' and 'A leaf'.

STEFFEN MENSCHING: to Mitteldeutscher Verlag and Agnes Stein (translator) for 'For Peter Weiss'; Mitteldeutscher Verlag and Margitt Lehbert (translator) for 'My coal merchant drives a Tatra', 'Your hair was drenched, 'Dreamlike excursion with Rosa L.', 'Jerry Mosololi (26), Simon Mogoerane (24), Marcus Motaung (28)' and 'In a hotel room in Meissen I read'.

CZESŁAW MIŁOSZ: to Penguin Books Ltd for extracts from 'Child of Europe', translated by Jan Darowski, in Czesław Miłosz, The Collected Poems 1931–1987 (Penguin Books, 1988), copyright © Czesław Miłosz Royalties, Inc., 1988.

ION MORAR: to Ion Morar and Oana Lungescu (translator) for

'The Trojan wave', 'One winter, one single day', 'Salt wins', 'Standard isolation' and 'The marquise went out at five o'clock'.

EWALD MURRER: to Ewald Murrer and Jarmila and Ian Milner (translators) for 'You are the one', 'There the journey begins', 'Twin skies' and 'Gifts'.

LYUBOMIR NIKOLOV: to Lyubomir Nikolov and Ewald Osers (translator) for 'Aladzha Monastery', 'Valley of the roses', 'Morning', 'Grandfather Nikola's oxen', 'The valley' and 'All day'.

IMRE ORAVECZ: to Imre Oravecz and Richard Aczel (translator) for 'In the beginning', 'I remember clearly', 'I'm trying to imagine you now', 'The sun is shining' and 'All I want' from *September 1972*, © Richard Aczel and Imre Oravecz.

ALEKSEI PARSHCHIKOV: to Aleksei Parshchikov and Michael Molnar (translator) for 'August on the Dnepr', 'Mudflats', 'Transfer' and 'New Year verses'.

GYÖRGY PETRI: to György Petri, *London Magazine* and George Gömöri and Clive Wilmer (translators) for 'Gratitude'; *Index on Censorship* and George Gömöri and Clive Wilmer for 'Night song of the personal shadow'; Anvil Press Poetry and George Gömöri and Clive Wilmer for 'By an unknown poet from Eastern Europe, 1955' from *Poetry World 2* (1988); George Gömöri and Clive Wilmer for 'Electra', 'To be said over and over again' and 'To Imre Nagy'.

JAN POLKOWSKI: to Jan Polkowski and Michael March and Jarosław Anders (translators) for 'The world is only air', 'I don't know that man', 'Bleeding breast', '*Noli me tangere*', 'Tell me' and 'Dusk'.

ZSUZSA RAKOVSZKY: to Zsuzsa Rakovszky and George Gömöri and Clive Wilmer (translators) for 'Snapshot', 'Noon', 'Evening', 'No longer' and 'Summer solistice'.

LUTZ RATHENOW: to Pfaffenweiler Presse and Agnes Stein (translator) for 'More notes on the theme of changing places', 'Dreams', 'Prague', 'To the poet Franz Kafka' and 'Faith'.

TOMAŽ ŠALAMUN: to Tomaž Šalamun; Tomaž Šalamun and Anselm Hollo (translators) for 'Proverbs' and 'Words', Tomaž Šalamun and Elliot Anderson (translators) for 'Jonah'; Charles Simic (translator) for 'Folk song' and 'Death's window'; Veno Taufer and Michael Scammell (translators) for 'Eclipse: II'.

ELENA SHVARTS: to Elena Shvarts; Bomb magazine and Michael Molnar (translator) for 'Animal-Flower' from Bomb magazine; Michael Molnar for 'Give me crimson ointment', 'Father butts in again', 'How could you dare', 'Claudia, you won't believe this' and 'How I envy you, Bacchantes!' – all from Cynthia.

IVO ŠMOLDAS: to Ivo Šmoldas and Jarmila and Ian Milner (translators) for 'Hour of the wolf', 'Winter children', 'Snapshot' and 'The flash'.

ELENA ȘTEFOI: to Elena Ștefoi and Oana Lungescu (translator) for 'Love letter', 'Very close to the horizon', 'Love poem as it may come off', 'Much later', 'Straight to Olympus you'll go' and 'This year in the month of March'.

LIVIU IOAN STOICIU: to Liviu Ioan Stoiciu and Oana Lungescu (translator) for 'Archaic mothers', 'From behind only the ashes', 'In windy twilight', 'From the tower watching', 'Resurrection' and 'Where space changes its meaning'.

JANA ŠTROBLOVÁ: to Jana Štroblová; Verse and Jarmila and Ian Milner (translators) for 'Circus' and 'The slaughterhouse'; Jarmila and Ian Milner for 'To whom shall we leave our souls', 'Skin' and 'The drought'.

NOVICA TADIĆ: to Novica Tadić and Michael March and Dušan Puvačić (translators) for 'The cats' strike', 'A small picture catalogue', 'At twilight', 'A conversation', 'The icicle' and 'Dice'.

EKATERINA YOSIFOVA: to Ekaterina Yosifova and Ewald Osers (translator) for 'Or the other way round'. 'Golden anchors', 'Increasing verbosity' and 'If I had not dissipated myself'.

TIBOR ZALÁN: to Tibor Zalán; Gerard Gorman (translator) for 'The wind the night the endless snowfall', 'I haven't told you yet' and 'The women we write poems about'; Daniel Hoffman (translator) for 'By dawn the shadows reach the windowsill'.

The publishers regret any errors or omissions and would be grateful to hear from any copyright holders not here fully acknowledged.

FOR THE BEST IN PAPERBACKS, LOOK FOR THE 🐧

In every corner of the world, on every subject under the sun, Penguin represents quality and variety – the very best in publishing today.

For complete information about books available from Penguin – including Puffins, Penguin Classics and Arkana – and how to order them, write to us at the appropriate address below. Please note that for copyright reasons the selection of books varies from country to country.

In the United Kingdom: Please write to *Dept E.P., Penguin Books Ltd, Harmondsworth, Middlesex, UB7 0DA.*

If you have any difficulty in obtaining a title, please send your order with the correct money, plus ten per cent for postage and packaging, to *PO Box No 11, West Drayton, Middlesex*

In the United States: Please write to *Dept BA, Penguin, 299 Murray Hill Parkway, East Rutherford, New Jersey 07073*

In Canada: Please write to *Penguin Books Canada Ltd, 2801 John Street, Markham, Ontario L3R 1B4*

In Australia: Please write to the *Marketing Department, Penguin Books Australia Ltd, P.O. Box 257, Ringwood, Victoria 3134*

In New Zealand: Please write to the *Marketing Department, Penguin Books (NZ) Ltd, Private Bag, Takapuna, Auckland 9*

In India: Please write to *Penguin Overseas Ltd, 706 Eros Apartments, 56 Nehru Place, New Delhi, 110019*

In the Netherlands: Please write to *Penguin Books Netherlands B.V., Postbus 195, NL–1380AD Weesp*

In West Germany: Please write to *Penguin Books Ltd, Friedrichstrasse 10–12, D–6000 Frankfurt/Main 1*

In Spain: Please write to *Longman Penguin España, Calle San Nicolas 15, E–28013 Madrid*

In Italy: Please write to *Penguin Italia s.r.l., Via Como 4, I-20096 Pioltello (Milano)*

In France: Please write to *Penguin Books Ltd, 39 Rue de Montmorency, F-75003 Paris*

In Japan: Please write to *Longman Penguin Japan Co Ltd, Yamaguchi Building, 2–12–9 Kanda Jimbocho, Chiyoda-Ku, Tokyo 101*

A SELECTION OF FICTION AND NON-FICTION

Perfume Patrick Süskind

It was after his first murder that Grenouille knew he was a genius. He was to become the greatest perfumer of all time, for he possessed the power to distil the very essence of love itself. 'Witty, stylish and ferociously absorbing' – *Observer*

A Confederacy of Dunces John Kennedy Toole

In this Pulitzer Prize-winning novel, in the bulky figure of Ignatius J. Reilly, an immortal comic character is born. 'I succumbed, stunned and seduced ... a masterwork of comedy' – *The New York Times*

In the Land of Oz Howard Jacobson

'The most successful attempt I know to grip the great dreaming Australian enigma by the throat and make it gargle' – *Evening Standard*. 'Sharp characterization, crunching dialogue and self-parody ... brilliantly funny' – *Literary Review*

Falconer John Cheever

Ezekiel Farragut, fratricide with a heroin habit, comes to Falconer Correctional Facility. His freedom is enclosed, his view curtailed by iron bars. But he is a man, none the less, and the vice, misery and degradation of prison change a man...

The Memory of War and Children in Exile: Poems 1968–83 James Fenton

'James Fenton is a poet I find myself again and again wanting to praise' – *Listener*. 'His assemblages bring with them tragedy, comedy, love of the world's variety, and the sadness of its moral blight' – *Observer*

The Bloody Chamber Angela Carter

In tales that glitter and haunt – strange nuggets from a writer whose wayward pen spills forth stylish, erotic, nightmarish jewels of prose – the old fairy stories live and breathe again, subtly altered, subtly changed.

The Book of Laughter and Forgetting Milan Kundera

'A whirling dance of a book ... a masterpiece full of angels, terror, ostriches and love ... No question about it. The most important novel published in Britain this year' – Salman Rushdie in the *Sunday Times*

Miami Joan Didion

'Joan Didion's Miami is at once an aggressively real city and a legendary domain to which Swift might well have posted Gulliver ... a work that combines intense imaginative vision with extraordinary argumentative force' – Jonathan Raban in the *Observer*

Milk and Honey Elizabeth Jolley

'In a claustrophobic family of Viennese refugees to Australia, the young boarder Jacob studies the cello, and is alternately pampered and terrified until his father dies and leaves him a fortune ... a quirky, brilliantly written study on the amorality of ignoring reality' – *The Times*

Einstein's Monsters Martin Amis

'This collection of five stories and an introductory essay ... announces an obsession with nuclear weapons; it also announces a new tonality in Amis's writing' – John Lanchester in the *London Review of Books*. 'He has never written to better effect' – John Carey in the *Sunday Times*

In the Heart of the Country J. M. Coetzee

In a web of reciprocal oppression in colonial South Africa, a white sheep-farmer makes a bid for salvation in the arms of a black concubine, while his embittered daughter dreams of and executes a bloody revenge. Or does she?

In Custody Anita Desai

Deven, a lecturer in a small town in northern India, is resigned to a life of mediocrity and empty dreams. Asked to interview Delhi's greatest poet, he discovers a new kind of dignity...

FOR THE BEST IN PAPERBACKS, LOOK FOR THE 🐧

PENGUIN BOOKS OF POETRY

American Verse
British Poetry Since 1945
Caribbean Verse in English
A Choice of Comic and Curious Verse
Contemporary American Poetry
Contemporary British Poetry
English Christian Verse
English Poetry 1918–60
English Romantic Verse
English Verse
First World War Poetry
Greek Verse
Irish Verse
Light Verse
Love Poetry
The Metaphysical Poets
Modern African Poetry
New Poetry
Poetry of the Thirties
Post-War Russian Poetry
Scottish Verse
Southern African Verse
Spanish Civil War Verse
Spanish Verse
Women Poets

FOR THE BEST IN PAPERBACKS, LOOK FOR THE 🐧

PENGUIN INTERNATIONAL WRITERS

Titles already published or in preparation

Gamal Al-Ghitany	**Zayni Barakat**
Isabel Allende	**Eva Luna**
Wang Anyi	**Baotown**
Joseph Brodsky	**Marbles: A Play in Three Acts**
Doris Dörrie	**Love, Pain and the Whole Damn Thing**
Shusaku Endo	**Scandal**
	Wonderful Fool
Ida Fink	**A Scrap of Time**
Daniele Del Giudice	**Lines of Light**
Miklos Haraszti	**The Velvet Prison**
Ivan Klíma	**My First Loves**
	A Summer Affair
Jean Levi	**The Chinese Emperor**
Harry Mulisch	**Last Call**
Cees Nooteboom	**The Dutch Mountains**
	A Song of Truth and Semblance
Milorad Pavić	**Dictionary of the Khazars**
Luise Rinser	**Prison Journal**
A. Solzhenitsyn	**Matryona's House and Other Stories**
	One Day in the Life of Ivan Denisovich
Tatyana Tolstoya	**On the Golden Porch and Other Stories**
Elie Wiesel	**Twilight**
Zhang Xianliang	**Half of Man is Woman**

FOR THE BEST IN PAPERBACKS, LOOK FOR THE 🐧

PENGUIN INTERNATIONAL POETS

Anna Akhmatova Selected Poems Translated by D. M. Thomas

Anna Akhmatova is not only Russia's finest woman poet but perhaps the finest in the history of western culture.

Fernando Pessoa Selected Poems

'I have sought for his shade in those Edwardian cafés in Lisbon which he haunted, for he was Lisbon's Cavafy or Verlaine' – Cyril Connolly in the *Sunday Times*

Yehuda Amichai Selected Poems
Translated by Chana Bloch and Stephen Mitchell

'A truly major poet ... there's a depth, breadth and weighty momentum in these subtle and delicate poems of his' – Ted Hughes

Czeslaw Miłosz Collected Poems 1931–1987
Winner of the 1980 Nobel Prize for Literature

'One of the greatest poets of our time, perhaps the greatest' – Joseph Brodsky

Joseph Brodsky To Urania
Winner of the 1987 Nobel Prize for Literature

Exiled from the Soviet Union in 1972, Joseph Brodsky has been universally acclaimed as the most talented Russian poet of his generation.

and

Tony Harrison Selected Poems
Philippe Jaccottet Selected Poems
Osip Mandelstam Selected Poems
Pablo Neruda Selected Poems